CAUGHT

THE SWAMP #3

REBECCA ROYCE

Caught (The Swamp #3)

Copyright @ 2020 by Rebecca Royce

Ebook ISBN: 978-1-951349-44-8

Print ISBN: 978-1-951349-51-6

Cover art by Syneca at Orignal Syn

Content Editing: Heather Long

Copy Editing: Jennifer Leigh Jones at Bookends Editing

Final Proof Editing: Meghan Leigh Daigle at Bookish Dreams Editing

Formatting: Ripley Proserpina

Published by Rebecca Royce

www.rebeccaroyce.com

❀ Created with Vellum

For Ripley Proserpina. -- I didn't kill off MacKenzie's whole family because you asked me not to.

FOREWORD

Dearest Reader,

Thank you so much for picking up Caught (The Swamp #3). I am so grateful to all of you who have gone on this ride with me. I have loved writing MacKenzie, Rainer, Preston, Jarret, and Anton. They have been like family to me. And I love how you love them.

So I'm not sure why I need to say this but for whatever reason every time I publish one of their novels, I receive hate messages afterwards. I thought the message telling me off that Hidden had a cliffhanger was bad but that was before the message came through on Facebook after Pursued telling me to stop writing. That one was such a bad hit that it threw me off my game for nearly a week. I couldn't write this book or any of my co-authored ones for days and days. Ultimately, I had to put this book away for months and write other things before I could come back to it.

I've never thought of myself as being thin-skinned. I take bad reviews really, really well. So this is what I would like to say to all of you today. I am a human, a real one. In addition to writing, I'm a mother of three, a wife, a friend, the vice president of communications for our local elementary school PTA, a pet owner, a movie lover... I could go on and on. We're all many things, right? As my mother would say, we all wear many hats.

The point being, I am a human being. And if you wouldn't say something to my face, please don't say it to me in a message. There are plenty of places for you to vent your spleen if you don't like a book—as is your right. Goodreads, anyone? Please do it there. Remember, authors are human.

My books aren't for everyone, but I truly appreciate you taking the time to read my words. I love my readers. I am grateful for every single one of you. Grateful to do this job. Lucky.

And now on to MacKenzie's happily ever after that I've been promising you from book one.

Thanks for giving me the chance to tell it,

Rebecca Royce

CHAPTER 1
PRESTON

There were times in my life that I never saw coming. Lately, it felt like every day was one. I stood to the side of the bed, watching Mac writhe on top of the covers. She talked to someone, but I had no idea with whom she held that conversation. We were losing her to madness. Every day, it got worse. Or at least, it seemed that way. This was only day two. Perhaps there would come a time when it would stop progressing. We hadn't hit that day yet.

A man named Ross Morgan was taking her piece by piece, until she'd stop communicating altogether. That was what happened to female werewolves when they became their version of the Loup. They faded into madness in their minds, unable to communicate with the outside world. But we weren't there yet. Bit by bit, we were losing our mate, and so far, there wasn't a fucking thing I could do about it.

Even through the closed windows, I could hear the sounds around me. More werewolves than I'd seen in decades swarmed through my house. They were here, a makeshift pack, to help my family fight this Loup who was after us. All of them had suffered. Yet, I had never loved huge crowds, even if they were pack, and their constant presence grated on my nerves like someone had taken a garlic peeler and tried to use it on my skin.

Beyond them, the sounds from outside warred with the scents I was desperate to get closer to. Forget that, what I really wanted was to scoop my mate off this bed and take her outside to the swamp with me. We were fucking home, but we weren't *home*. And all I wanted in the world was to get her to where she could really be *home* with us.

I stalked to the window, taking a deep breath. This was where my family had always lived, until the Accords screwed everything up. We were meant to be here. I could smell the deer, the raccoons, the alligators, frogs, and turtles. Fuck, I could even smell the snakes. All of it called to my wolf, begging me to shift, but all my wolf wanted was my mate. Healthy. Happy. Here.

The door opened and closed, and my younger brother Jarret entered. Without a word, he walked to the edge of the bed and scooted in next to Mac. Wrapping her in his arms, he held her like he would never let her go.

We all had our ways in life. He wanted to cuddle, to heal. I wanted to rage. But at the end of the day, we were both stuck with no way out of this mess.

The phone rang in my pocket, and I picked it up before it could bother Mac. Although, I would love to see her eyes open. They hadn't done that yet today.

"Yeah?" Yes, I was answering the phone that way. Anyone who called instead of texted would get that kind of annoyance right now.

"That's how you say hello?" It was Rainer. I'd never been so happy to hear my big brother's voice in my life. Truth was, we'd been close most of our lives, until it all fell apart when he went to jail. These days, he was more than my trusted friend and relative, he was my pack leader, and we shared a mate.

He'd been hauled off by the police and worrying about him was my second most concerning thing at the moment. Rainer could handle himself. He wasn't being attacked psychically by a sick wolf who I might have had sympathy for, if he hadn't come after what was mine.

"Talk." I hoped he could hear what he'd certainly smell if he were here. I was the on the edge of losing my mind.

"I'm on my way back. The cops don't even know why they have me here. Looks like Ross can mind control humans, too."

I winced. "The hits just keep on coming. So we can't even be sure the humans we don't want to deal with in the first place aren't working for Ross."

"We kind of knew anyway." Rainer was quiet for a second. "That's how he got all of those people to attack us to begin with."

"Sure." I lifted my mouth off the phone to speak to Jarret. "Big brother's okay."

He held up his thumb in the universal sign for good. It was like he was up-voting us. I swore he spent three times the amount of time online that I did, liking things or whatever. I only cared about social media in as much as it helped with my business. The same job that was probably gone now, since I hadn't set foot inside the building or seen any of the employees or boats in I didn't know how long.

Oh well. Starting over would just have to be the name of the game.

"How is she?"

I regarded Mac for a long second before I answered him. "She's not awake, but she's not sleeping." The acrid smell of pain assaulted my nose, as though speaking about her made me even more conscious of the situation. "She's not doing well."

Rainer audibly sighed. "As you are the king of under-playing things, I'm going to take that for just as bad as it must be. I'm on my way home. I borrowed this phone from my driver."

"You're with a driver, and you're talking about humans as though you aren't one?"

He laughed. I was glad one of us still could. "He's a wolf. I knew him back when I worked as a chef. He was a waiter in the restaurant. Anyway, he's coming with me. Wants to join the pack. Heard we're shifting. It's apparently all anyone is talking about."

"Interesting." I actually didn't care if he brought back hundreds of former waiters turned drivers. I supposed numbers were better than not. Even if I wanted all of them out of my house yesterday. I sighed. No, what got me was that Rainer had just suggested that we had a pack. When had that become something he'd accepted? Last I'd heard, he railed against it.

He said something to the man driving and then back to me. "Tell her I'm coming."

I shook my head, not that he could see that. "I'm not sure it'll matter. She can't hear us right now. Wherever her mind has gone…it's not here with us."

"Fuck."

To say the least. "Yep. See you soon."

I disconnected the phone. Jarret's eyes were closed, and he was asleep now, holding her like she was his pillow and he needed her to get through the night. Part of me was willing to climb in next to them and cuddle, too. But that wasn't how I functioned. Not really. Not when there were things to be done.

Leaving her in Jarret's loving arms, I exited the room quietly. The dull roar of noise greeted me even stronger, which showed me just how good the doors to my room were at canceling noise. This was an old house. Sometimes, older was just made better.

I took the stairs two at a time, ignoring everyone, even Miranda, who was an Alpha wolf who had saved our asses. I just couldn't talk. Not to anyone right then.

My mate was slipping through my hands, and I was powerless to help.

I'd even googled Ross Morgan to see if I could come up with anything. He had to be super rich. Surely, there couldn't be that many Ross Morgans running around who had that kind of power and influence to fund the things he was doing. Nothing.

The building we'd raided in Atlanta, where we'd found everyone, was registered to an LLC that was connected to an offshore account I couldn't yet infiltrate. This was like super spy shit, and I couldn't compete. I was a werewolf. A swamp rat. A small business owner. No fucking way was I supposed to be playing at this level.

I knew how to kill. How to protect. I didn't know how to fix this. How to save her. I was lost.

I'd never been a crier, and I wouldn't indulge now. Mac deserved better than that from me. Focus.

I pulled off my shirt, even as I was out the front door, shifting into my wolf body. I needed moments to collect myself. Then I'd return and be back to her.

If Mac were conscious, she'd tell me to do this. To settle. To be the wolf. Or some shit. She was a healer. An Omega. This was what she did. She'd put her hands on me and heal me from the inside out. I'd watched her push a bullet out of Jarret with nothing more than her mind and her hands on his body. She'd turned us all around from the control Ross Morgan had on us. The woman was nothing less than a miracle. My miracle.

And I was a total failure in helping her.

Fully shifted, I rushed into the forest around the swamp. The heat hit me differently than it did in my human form. I craved this. My vision tunneled. There was a rabbit nearby. What a stupid fucking rabbit to hang around in the vicinity of so many werewolves.

I wasn't interested in hunting. Not then. What I needed was to run. I'd had enough blood, had enough fighting. I had to run until I could think, until I could come up with the Hail Mary pass that would save the love of my life.

So help me, I would not lose her to madness. I would not lose our happy future with her. We needed to just be allowed to be. I growled at the thought.

A scent caught my attention, and I turned to face the wolf who had come to invade my solitary run. I knew Anton's as well as I did anyone. My brother who had been silenced by Morgan and his ilk when he was just a baby. They'd taken his fucking vocal cords.

There he was, staring at me through his wolf eyes. How long had he been out here? I didn't know. Anton had always done his own thing. Whether that was a natural tendency, or because he'd been rendered mute and my mother had refused to help him communicate out of some fucked up need to believe he'd eventually be fine, I didn't know. We'd never know.

He loved our mate with an intensity that matched my own. And right then, he was exactly what I needed.

Anton was here. That was great. We were going to fucking run.

Taking off as fast and mindlessly as I could, I ran against Anton's speed. I ran against his pain. I ran, knowing he'd chase and maybe beat me because he could feel it, too. If ever there was a person who knew what this hole in my chest felt like, it was Anton. We were fighters. And we had no enemy to challenge, no battle to win.

Pack. Mate. They were everything, they were life. All of it dissolved while I stood with nothing to do.

That damned Loup. Why hadn't some pack eliminated him when he first changed to the madness? We hunted the lone wolves who lost it. That was what we did.

Well...used to do. Until Morgan changed all that by pushing the Accords and somehow stopping us from having Omegas.

If I ever saw him, I might ask him how he'd done that. Then I'd tear out his throat.

I didn't know how long we ran. Anton was a great partner for this. He kept up, sometimes pulling ahead, sometimes falling behind. There were new smells—alligators, snakes, flowers—that came and went. We were far from home. He must have realized that we'd gone too long at the same time I did, because we both skidded to a stop, panting.

Mac was too far away. I nodded my head at him before I bumped him in the side. We'd run back. That would have to be enough.

Anton shook his head, and I stopped. He nodded up toward the moon, and I followed his gaze. It was full tonight. Why did he want me to see that? Full moons had nothing to do with our lives. Not really. We were werewolves when the moon was full, we were werewolves when it wasn't. What difference did it make? It was pretty, but I'd rather go after a gator if he needed to do something else before we returned.

I blinked. Hold on. Anton was incredibly smart, probably the most intellectually superior of any of us. All the time we wasted arguing and talking about nothing, he was forever thinking of things we never considered.

Why was he indicating the moon? What did that mean?

Fuck me. The Loups were affected by the moon. The rest of us, no. But they couldn't help their shifts during that time. They had to. That was part of what made them so dangerous. Exposure.

Ross Morgan—whatever superior Loup he was—needed to shift tonight.

And must have every full moon for however long this had been going on for him.

He was old. We knew that much. At some point, that fucker had probably been caught. Humans didn't know what to do when they ran into proof of us. They freaked out. Sometimes, they took to social media. The Accords couldn't stop the Loups. Not that there were too many of them around anymore, but before we'd all shut off the best parts of ourselves, there had been wolves whose job it had been to take care of exposure. My father, Cristian, had been one of them for a while.

I took off running toward the house. It was going to be time consuming and mind numbing, but so help me, I would place money that I could find this asshole by just following his crumbs. Sighting after sighting, I'd go through all of them until he was mine.

I shifted as I hit the porch. I'd made the run back in record time with Anton right on my heels. Swinging around, I stared at my brother. We were both out of breath. "Thanks."

He nodded before he placed his hand over his heart.

Yeah...that's what she was. Our heart.

I grabbed a pair of sweatpants that we'd started storing on the porch to take care of the nudity-after-shifts problem and stormed into the house. I'd figure out a shirt later. Right now, I was too hot for one anyway. I stormed into my office.

Mac's brothers were in there, but they both jumped up like they were ready for orders as soon as I entered.

"How is she?" Agustin asked first.

I shook my head. "Currently not verbal. Which might be better because she smells like pain."

I'd had more than enough of that scent from her. We'd finally gotten her back from the agony of losing her mating marks. When this was all over, Mac was going to be warm, well-fed, well-loved, and happy every day of her life.

Or as close to that as I could make it.

Her happiness and well-being were going to be my main objectives in life. And if she didn't make it through this... well, there would be big steps taken then, too. I wasn't living a life without her, so there was just no choice but to get through this and come out the other end.

"We have to seek out information on werewolf sightings. I don't believe the Loup is moving around. He has a central spot. We have to find it."

Agustin's eyes lit up. "Great idea."

I nodded toward Anton. "It was his."

My brother, shirtless like me, nodded. He held up the laptop computer on the desk. We needed more than just his tablet and my laptop. I had a pack full of werewolves. They all wanted to participate? Great. I'd put them to work.

"Agustin, take the cars. Go out and buy as many devices as you can on the credit card you'll find in the drawer over there. It's my work account. I'll take up my misuse of the account with the IRS later. Buy the store out. And then order more to be delivered tomorrow. I want everyone on this. We're seeking a place that keeps reporting werewolf sightings. This might take some time, but it's doable. I know it is."

Her brother squeezed my arm. "We'll save my sister."

We would. And then we were going to kill this fucker. Slowly.

I did love to play with my prey.

———

MacKenzie

I walked toward the end of the dock. I'd been stuck here for days. I couldn't seem to leave. Whenever I turned around to do so, I kept ending up back on this dock. It was so strange. I couldn't remember getting here, I couldn't remember even where I'd been before here.

It was like I'd always existed on this dock.

Only, that wasn't right. It couldn't be. Could it?

"Why did you leave me to die?"

The man was back. I sniffed the air. He was a werewolf like me.

I'd seen him before. He was frequently on this dock with me. But this was the first time he'd spoken. Or at least, I thought it was. I couldn't be sure. My memory was...tricky.

"I don't recall leaving you to die. I'm not sure I know who you are. I'm not sure I know who I am, and it seems... unlikely I left you to die. Right?"

I had the feeling this wasn't the first time my memory had gone askew. Why would that be? I wasn't sure.

"You all left me. All of you Omegas. You left me to die"

Omegas? Should I know what that was?

Jarret

My mother used to say the problem with me was that I over-thought everything. I couldn't make decisions because I couldn't decide what would happen to an absolute certainty. I'd see too many sides of too many issues. If I did A, B would happen, and I wasn't sure I wanted B. Then I'd decide I did want it, but not outcome C. She used to say that I spent so much time thinking with my head, that I'd made no room for my heart in any decisions.

The sad truth was that my mother was very often wrong, and in this case, she'd gotten that totally off base. The trouble with me wasn't that I overthought things; it was that I couldn't stop thinking about them. That came straight from my heart. I never wanted to let anyone down. I wanted to be everything for everyone.

So I couldn't let things go.

But lately, I'd been convinced that it made me stronger. I understood how to connect to others in a way I wasn't sure my brothers did.

What was more was that Kenzie didn't mind those sides of me. She seemed to love me just as I was. Mates really were a miraculous thing.

I chewed on my lip. In my arms, she twitched and muttered unintelligible things. My wolf clawed inside my skin. I'd known it the second Preston and Anton had left the house. I completely understood the inclination. It would feel good to give my animal something to do rather than obsess.

Still, I'd stay right here. They'd have to pry my dead body away from Kenzie. I wasn't leaving her, not for a second, not until she was better. Even then, it might be hard for her to get me to go.

I'd been lost in my own head when Kenzie had brought me back. There was a certain irony to that. Or maybe not.

Preston had been sent to capture her. He was aggressive, unrelenting. Rainer, he'd been out leading missions to do who knew what. My oldest brother was a natural leader. He could get all of us to do amazing things. Anton, they'd silenced and yet used his brain. He'd managed to beat them at their own game, leaving messages in his published works that Mac and Preston used to free all of us.

But what about me? What did it mean that I'd been so lost in my own head, resistant to what they'd done to me? Did that even matter, or was I, once again, overthinking things?

I shook my head. No, I wasn't. I had to trust myself. I knew more than I'd ever imagined I did.

I could connect to people. I was good at it.

Could I do that with Kenzie right now?

Could I reach her?

With Rainer away, there was no one I had to ask before I tried. He'd never appointed a second, and although Preston might be it by default, I doubted he wanted the role. Leading wasn't really his thing.

I sat up, drawing her closer to me. As gently as I could, I pressed our foreheads together. "Kenzie, you are a healer. You reached me in the darkest of places. Brought me back. Now, if there is any part of you that can feel me, any part of you that still has your power, still has the ability to hear me, bring me to you."

Nothing happened. I supposed the smart thing to do, the

sensible next step, would be to stop. To get on with getting on. But I couldn't do that.

"Come on, Kenzie. Let me in. Please."

I'd beg if it would help. Get down on my knees and plead for hours. Days. Years.

For a second, I felt like I floated. A long tunnel led to a dock... A dock? I looked around. Where was I? That was when I spotted her.

She stood at the end of the dock, someone next to her.

I rushed forward, or attempted to. My legs wouldn't work. I fought against my immobility, desperate to reach my love. Still, nothing changed. Wherever this was, I couldn't walk around here.

"Kenzie," I shouted out, hoping she'd hear me, holding out my arms to her. "Kenzie."

She and the man standing with her both turned. He narrowed his gaze at me, while she stared at me blankly, not saying a word.

"What are you doing here?" he yelled. "You don't belong here."

With a rush, I was back in my body, the dock, Kenzie, and that man all gone. I panted like I'd been running. Anton stared down at me, his shirt half on, concern evident on his features. He held up his tablet.

You okay? I was worried about you. The mechanical voice spoke for him.

"I was with her. On a dock." It was hard to explain.

Dreaming?

I shook my head quickly. "No, I asked her to bring me where she was. She did. I could see her. Not get to her. But speak to her. She's there with some man. I bet it's Ross Morgan. And she had no idea what was going on, or maybe even who I was. Anton, it was real."

I'm going to go tell Preston. We're working on locating him. Maybe the dock is real. Maybe we should be trying to look for places with bodies of water. Good work.

Anton rushed off. I smiled. Maybe I had helped. Maybe I'd done something to make things better. I kissed Kenzie's hand, loving the feel of her soft skin. "We're coming for you. I swear that we are. Stay there and wait for us."

Only silence and her moving mouth, lost to her madness, answered me. When I found Ross Morgan, I was going to drown him in that water. After I let him bleed for a while for taking what was mine.

CHAPTER 2

RAINER

"You okay, Alpha?"

I blinked. Took me a hot second to realize he was talking to me. That was going to take some getting used to. I'd never aimed to be anyone's Alpha, ever. Not even when I'd been the golden boy looking just like my Alpha bio-father. Kevin was Alpha. I was happy being just me. Hell, the truth was I wasn't Alpha. I might get to lead because I was the oldest Lejeune brother, but MacKenzie was our leader. Hands down. She was the Omega, and that pretty much made her Alpha in my book. Whatever she wanted, whatever she needed. Her word was my law. Except when I had to yank her back in battle.

My mate couldn't be at risk. First and foremost, because I loved her more than I loved anything. Second, because she was the only living Omega. But she was brave and stubborn. Wanted me to be the Alpha I'd been born to be, lowered her eyes when it suited her, and fought me like hell when it didn't. I smiled at the thought. I loved her fucking spirit.

"I'm fine. Lots on my mind. Thanks for checking."

He nodded. The boy was nervous. I could smell it. He

didn't know quite what to do, had never shifted, wanted it more than he wanted to breathe, and now needed me to instruct him how. In normal circumstances, I'd love this more than anything. Training our people how to be who they were always supposed to be seemed like a worthy life for me. If I could figure out how to cook for people, too, while loving on my mate every possible second, that would be all I needed in life.

But those weren't options.

No, I had to figure out how to save MacKenzie from a Loup who had it out for her, and I was going to have to lead a bunch of werewolves who thought I was their Alpha because I was with her. My hands itched. I wanted—no, needed—to shift, but it wasn't going to be happening anytime soon. I had to sit in this car because that stupid human-controlling Loup was making our life hell.

My fangs threatened to descend, and I held them back. This wasn't what I was made for. Give me a target, and I'd take it down. But this whole larger than life thing with an enemy I couldn't touch... I didn't know how to do this.

"Now might be the wrong time to tell you this, kid. But we're under constant attack, and there's a Loup who is somehow like the Lex Luthor of Loups and is making everything hell. He's got my mate, who is the Omega, trapped in madness. And he's controlling humans and wolves alike to attack us all the time. If you don't want to step into this, it might be the time to drop me and go."

He shook his head. "Oh...no I'm in. But...is a... What's it called?"

I didn't have the slightest idea what he was talking about. "Sorry, I'm not following."

"Is he an Alpha who went Loup? Because my mother used to call that the Alpha Loup. She told it to me like it was a fairy tale, right? Or like humans talk about their ancestors. Once upon a time in the old country kind of a thing. I don't know much about it, just that those were considered to be really, really bad. Because they have all the Alpha qualities. But they're also Loup, so they're out of control."

My mind whirled. I wasn't sure I'd ever heard this story. We weren't a really big storytelling family. Even when we'd lived in the swamp, we'd been sort of political. Handling everybody's problems in the pack. Threats. My mother wasn't ever the huggy, kissy type who rocked us to sleep with stories. An Alpha going Loup? How did that even work? It was lone wolves who went Loup. An Alpha?

"Can I use your phone again?"

He handed it back to me, and I nodded at him in thanks. But before I picked it up, I owed this kid thanks and the courtesy of at least learning his name. "Remind me your name. I should know it. I've never been great with names. It's a problem, I know. I can promise you that I'll always know your scent."

To a non-shifter, that would sound weird. Truth was the way the guy carried the scent of motor oil and mint, coupled with his natural aroma, would stay with me. It had always been that way for me, but now that I was regularly shifting again, it was even more so.

"I don't know that I ever told you, actually. I'm Donovan."

I'd remember it now. "Donovan, you may have saved the day. Maybe."

My mind churned. An Alpha becoming a Loup? I dialed Preston and waited. He didn't answer. Fuck me. Did I know Jarret's number? I hoped I did. It was amazing I knew Preston's, considering how little we'd spoken over the last years. The good news about Preston was he so rarely changed anything. He'd had the same one since he first got the phone. Not that it was doing me any fucking good right now.

I dialed what I hoped was Jarret's number, and after two rings he picked up. "Hello?"

He sounded like I'd woken him. "Sleeping?"

"Not really. I was... I kind of broke into Kenzie's head. It's hard to describe. She drew me in. I saw her. With a man on a dock. Where are you?"

I looked around, not entirely sure how to answer that. "In the car. Probably about an hour out."

"Good. We need you. I don't know exactly what we're doing, but I know we need you."

His words panged what I would have at one time called my nonexistent heart. We'd never been close. I still wasn't one hundred percent sure I understood Jarret. There were parts of him I'd never get. But MacKenzie seemed to understand him, and for that, I was grateful. When I was doing hard time, I certainly never thought my brothers would need me or want me around. Our mate had saved us all.

"Do you know anything about Alphas becoming Loups?"

He was quiet for a second. "No. Not at all. Why? This is a thing? Is Ross an Alpha?"

"Dude, I don't know." I sighed. "Who would know?"

"Oh." I could practically hear Jarret sitting up as he spoke. "Miranda's here. She's driving Preston crazy. Wants to talk. You know Pres, he doesn't want to talk."

No, he really didn't want to, hardly ever. "She's perfect. You have the number?"

"Yeah, it came up on my phone. Whose number is it anyway?"

I smiled. Leave it to Jarret to just clue in. "His name is

Donovan. Can you give this number to Miranda and ask her to call me?"

"On it."

I hung up and sat back in the car. I was Alpha-ing in the car. It was like modern Alphahood or some shit. Donovan was clearly a smart kid. He kept his mouth shut and drove. He'd given me information I might or might not be able to use, and I was grateful to him.

There was a lot to uncover here. At some time, I was going to ask Jarret to better describe what he meant by being dragged into MacKenzie's dreams. What did that even mean? How had she done that? One of the last things she'd told us was that she was losing her powers. Was that not true?

The phone rang, and I picked it up, even though it was Donovan's. Maybe I had more Alpha in me than I thought. Technically, if I was his Alpha, then all he had belonged to me anyway. Not that I'd ever take people's stuff just to have it. What a repugnant thought.

"Hello?" I stared out the window, hoping I wasn't about to have to talk to Donovan's mother.

"Rainer? You okay?" It was Miranda's voice.

All right, now we were getting somewhere. "I got through it. I think the men I talked to are somewhat confused, but they'll do what humans always do and get on with it, not thinking too much about what they don't understand. Humans are great about forgetting."

"You've got that right. Unfortunately, those who don't are also great about killing."

I grunted my consent. "You're fine?"

Pleasantries weren't really my thing, but she was an Alpha. I couldn't talk to her with anything but respect. "Everyone is agog here, researching Loup sightings that correlate with bodies of water. Although it might just be a tiny lake here, so we're probably chasing our tails, so to speak."

I rolled my eyes at the imagery. I'd never chased my tail in my life. "I have a question."

"Go on," she said fast.

Well, I would have done that if she hadn't interrupted me to begin with. "Do you know any legends about Alpha Loups?"

"Of course, but they're just legends. Alphas don't become Loups. Only lone wolves."

I took a long breath. "What if that's not true? What if the fact that this one can do all the things he can do is because he never was your typical Loup to begin with? What if he was an Alpha to begin with? All the ways you can control your pack, all the ways that you do things, take the Loup factor and you have Ross. Alphas can live a long time. Maybe that's how he's done this... Like, he's Louped all of us. Alpha'd all of us or some shit."

She was so quiet, I wondered if she'd lost the connection, but at last, she spoke. "My skin is tingling. I think you're right. I think this is right. You're really on to something here. How did you come upon this?"

I stared at Donovan driving. "It's good to have pack."

"It sure is. You know what this means, right?" I could hear conversation going on in the background. I needed to be there, not in this car. Patience had never been my strong suit.

"No, Miranda. I don't know, unfortunately." I wasn't really annoyed at her, but keeping it from seeping into my voice was going to be a test I was unfortunately losing.

A car passed us fast on the right. I growled. We were going eighty miles an hour. That asshole was going to kill someone. She finally answered me. "He needs to be Alpha challenged."

"Well, as soon as we find him, you can go ahead and do that, Miranda. I'll even applaud."

She laughed, a loud sound that stopped all the talking behind her. "Oh no, darling Rainer. This one? This one belongs to you."

I hung up the phone. She was right. This one was mine. I was taking down that Loup. Alpha to Alpha. I might not have wanted the job, but now that I had it, I'd eat him alive. Drinking his blood while I did so. My mouth watered.

MacKenzie

I watched the shouting man I didn't know as he disappeared. I had no idea who he was. Or did I? I rubbed my eyes. Things were sort of confusing. Still, I was having sort of an important conversation, and as long as I had to be caught here, I might as well finish having it.

"What do you mean, we let you down? How did we do that?" I reached out to touch the man's arm. He was in pain. I burned to do something to help him, but I wasn't sure what that was exactly. What could I do?

He visibly swallowed. "I was in so much pain. So much. And the Omegas didn't help me. Why didn't they help me? That's why...that's why the second I could, I got rid of them all. I am Alpha. I decide what happens. Even with the humans. They don't know I can control them, but I do. And every werewolf ever born. I am the strongest of them all."

I dropped my hand. Something about that just felt wrong. The water looked lovely, serene, almost too much. As though I needed to throw a pebble into it to make ripples, just so that it would be less perfect. Instead, I sat down on the edge of the dock and stared forward.

"Don't ignore me!" he shouted.

I turned toward him. "I'll be happy to speak to you when you are not saying ridiculous things. If you want me to answer, stop saying braggadocious things. I don't have a clue what you're talking about anyway. It all seems like nonsense."

His face became a shade of orange reminiscent of a pumpkin. Yes, he didn't like what I'd said, and much as my hands burned and I wanted to do...something...I didn't really care that he was having a temper tantrum. Any second now, he might stomp his foot.

Instead, he sat down next to me. "You not remembering things is actually a gift I'm giving you. I'm afraid you might go insane if I let you know what is going on."

MacKenzie...

Whose voice was that talking to me?

I'm home, baby. We're going to get this taken care of.

I felt like I should know that voice the way that I should have known the man who was here temporarily. Only I didn't.

"You've done something to me. That much I understand. In the same way I know this place isn't real. Nothing is this beautiful, this serene. If you want to talk to me, it should be on equal footing. Give me back what you took from me, so that I know you as well as you know me, and we can go from there. Until then? Sorry. I'm going to sit here and think about nothing... I'll contemplate my belly button for hours. I don't care. I'm not doing this with you anymore."

He widened his eyes. "You shouldn't be able to summon that kind of temper. Not here."

"I may not know much about myself, but I do know that I've got a backbone, and I'm not afraid to use it. So do you want to talk, or do you want to sit here? I'm good with either. But if you want to get anywhere with me, cut the crap already."

———

Anton

Sometimes, it was frustrating not knowing what was real, what I'd made up in my head, and what had been planted there in the years that Ross Morgan had fucked with my life. I shouldn't even have been thinking of that in past tense. The man was still fucking with my life.

Now it was in the shape of taking my mate from me, stealing her mind.

I'd do anything to protect her from this.

Who in the world would have thought I'd even have a mate? Me, the broken Lejeune. The man without a voice. My mother hid me from the world, not letting me see people outside of our small inner circle, terrified every second that something would happen to me. There were days I'd considered hopping out the window, disappearing, and never coming back.

But then I'd thought of Preston and how he'd always had my back, always seen to it that I was treated like everyone else, how it would hurt him if I did that, and I'd stayed. Jarret had been around, too. Now that I understood he blamed himself, much of our earlier relationship made sense. And Rainer? Well, I'd worshiped him. Not that he'd known it. He'd always seemed larger than life to me, like our fathers.

I'd never thought I'd have a mate, let alone that she would be the one and only Omega. Or that she would smell like springtime and understand what I wanted to say without me needing to speak. How was that possible?

The second I'd seen her, when Gus brought her into the house, I'd simply known. I'd never shifted in my life, never been a werewolf, and yet it was like all of those instincts were right where they were supposed to be. I'd scented her, then I'd seen her and boom...she was mine. Hadn't surprised me she was theirs, too. Much as we were the most dysfunctional bunch of werewolves ever born to a family, we were always meant to be together. Who else was going to put up with us?

My beautiful mate loved us all.

I scanned through my books. I'd never in a million years have imagined that I would encode inside the pages messages to myself and others to explain this craziness. How had I even done this? How strong a connection did I have to this Loup? Could I become one myself?

Being silent meant I had lots of time to think, since I had no desire to try to make my ideas understood to those who didn't want to take five seconds to let me get them out. My brothers, fine. They seemed to be willing to pause, but the rest of the bunch searching the Internet with Preston could all go jump in a ditch. They whispered about me and never took the time to know the man they spent all that time discussing.

It was bothersome but low on my list of things I worried about.

We needed a lake. I'd written about one. Hadn't I? What did it mean that I couldn't really remember? They were my books. Shouldn't I have known them inside and out? And yet there had always been a distance I'd felt in regards to them. As though someone else had written them.

Now I sort of understood why. Maybe I wasn't talented. Maybe I was just some kind of conduit.

Questions for another time.

I wasn't finding anything I needed here.

Rainer leaned against the doorway, watching me. Jarret was upstairs with our mate, where I'd like to be if I had a choice, but I didn't. Preston had become mister organizer. Who would have thought it? And my big brother was back.

I'd scented his arrival, heard him come in, and hadn't blamed him in the least when he'd headed straight upstairs to our mate.

"Seems you saved the day." Rainer strode toward me. "Thank you."

I nodded. Even if I could speak, there wouldn't be more to say than that. Yes, I'd come up with the idea about the Loups being spotted. But Preston had taken it to a whole other level. We were a team, and I was grateful we were all in this together.

"Need help? I can't get near a computer to help any of them. Besides, I think my role in this is going to somehow be to Alpha challenge the Loup when we find him."

I jolted. Was that a thing? Was Morgan an Alpha? That meant there was an explanation for how he controlled us. All the years running amok in my head was because he'd been...what...my Alpha? I hadn't consented to that. There was a give and take between the Alphas and everyone else. We had to want to be with them. Their dominance made that happen, but still, I'd been a baby way too young to agree to anything. Fuck. It was like a mind rape.

Rainer placed his hand on my shoulder, and I jumped.

"You okay? Where'd you go? Nowhere good."

I hugged him. We weren't really huggy people, but I was so glad he was here, so glad he was Alpha, so glad to share MacKenzie with him. If anyone could save her, could save all of us, it was Rainer. He just didn't know it. The Accords and council had broken him. What was worse was I was pretty sure the council had done it on purpose. Break the strong, make them weak, knock them down.

But she was bringing him back. She was doing that for all of us.

He patted my back. "It's been a lot. And we've had no time to deal with any of it, little brother. You keep coming through. You always do."

I hoped I could continue to do so. I waved my hand over the mess on my desk. So far, I was getting nowhere.

He looked over it. "Do you make notes anywhere, or do you just write directly on the page?"

I jolted. Fuck. Yes, I made notes. I used to do it more than I did lately, but when I first started writing, I saw so many scenes in my head I could barely contain myself. There had been notebooks. But I didn't have them here. I grabbed the tablet.

"Back at the house in New Orleans." The computer spoke for me.

He winced. "Just got back from there. We need those notebooks. Can you take the car and go back and get them?"

I nodded. That I could do. No problem. Without conscious thought as to why I looked up at the ceiling. She was right upstairs, right above our heads. My love. My heart. My everything.

Rainer sat down in the chair. "She'll be okay. I won't settle for less."

How did he not know he was Alpha? I shook my head. It didn't matter. He would be when it counted.

Where were my keys? He held them up, and I grinned. Yeah, he knew me.

Stepping out of the quiet of the office to the chaos of the living room, I knew why Rainer had sought me out. Preston was in the center, barking orders. He took a long pull of a bottle of water. They were going to solve this, and I was going to help them. I just had to get to New Orleans and back with nothing going wrong.

CHAPTER 3
PRESTON

I had a list of five places. That was so much better than where we'd started. I sat back in my chair. Fuck. I really wasn't cut out for this. I was a wolf. Give me something to hunt and kill, I'd get that done. These incremental movements were killing me. Let the cats stalk, I wanted to attack. I sat back in my chair. Maybe I was just a lousy wolf.

Rainer's scent hit me, and I spun around to see him. I knew he'd gotten back, smelled and heard it, but he hadn't come to see me yet.

My older brother was all Alpha in that moment. I wasn't sure I could explain the difference, how and when it worked. Sometimes, Rainer didn't come across like we all needed to follow him, like he was always in charge. He'd been born for it and seemed on track to take the position for years. Then prison happened, and it changed him, broke him.

But like everything else our Omega did, she'd gotten him back to the place where I could see him again. And yeah...I wanted to follow him right now.

The room quieted. Everyone's gazes moved from what they were doing to stare at Rainer. That was saying a lot, considering Miranda was here and she gave off the same *look at me* vibes. But right now, Rainer's were stronger.

Interesting.

I got to my feet. "Brother."

He put his arm on mine. "Thanks for keeping things under control here. I'm going to go see her in a second. Wanted to tell you Anton had a thought and I sent him to go collect notebooks from New Orleans."

I nodded. There was a time I would have worried about Anton doing that alone, but these days, I understood that Anton might actually be the strongest out of all of us. He could do pretty much anything. "Jarret is proving to have some pretty incredible psychic wolf talents."

"Not surprising. He's always been untapped in his abilities." Rainer rubbed his eyes. "This was smart thinking, trying to look at the reports. Good work with this."

I shrugged. "Anton, too."

"Rainer, can I see you please?" Miranda wanted his attention, and I stepped back to get onto my computer. There were a few more things to check, and if the Alpha wanted to talk, then I'd let them do it.

My brother's eyes turned wolf for a second, and he took a long breath. "Later."

He turned his back on Miranda and headed upstairs, leaving her standing there. What was that about? I went back to my seat. I didn't need to be in the middle of that mess. Miranda waited a second before she took off toward the kitchen. I quickly glanced between them before I went back to ignoring what had happened. I had enough things to concern myself with without getting into some Alpha thing with them.

Who was going to talk to who on whose terms? It was going to turn out to be some shit like that.

I cracked my neck and looked over the computer again. What had I been doing?

All around me, the sounds of typing and clicking filled the air. When had we gotten so many chairs? With the amount of people we had around here, it had become a place I hardly recognized. Not like the swamp outside. Houses became homes in no time flat, they changed to fit the people in them. Packs were like that, too. Add a member, and the way it felt to be in them could be entirely different.

I understood the ins and outs of it. I just hated having to focus on the details. I lifted my hands from the keys. *The details.*

What did we know about Ross? He employed humans. There were paper trails for that. I employed small numbers, and it was endless paperwork. Morgan must be paying taxes. I growled at the humanness of it.

I was going to talk to my lawyer. He'd know how to find someone who didn't want to be found. The trouble was that I didn't have his number here. I had it locked in my work cell phone in my desk at the swamp tour office.

Great. It was a perfectly valid excuse to get out of the house and my would-be pack.

"Hey," I spoke to the guy sitting next to me. What was his name? Tony...maybe? I needed to pay better attention to these things. Or fuck it. Maybe I didn't. This was Rainer's domain. I was the eccentric, reclusive brother. He could figure out names, give everyone a tag to wear if he wanted to. "If anyone needs a break, make sure they know it's okay to take one."

Were we going to have meetings with this forming pack? Hi, my name is Preston, and this week...

I shuddered. He'd better not make our pack like that. All I wanted was my mate and my brothers. Everyone else would be peripheral. Not that I wasn't grateful all of these strangers were helping me get my mate free of this nightmare. Of course, she'd saved all of them. It would be pretty shitty if they hadn't helped.

I jumped in my car. I could take the airboat and reach the offices via swamp, but I didn't want to draw that kind of attention to myself if anyone was watching. Everyone drove, it wouldn't make anyone watching take notice that I'd gotten on the boat.

My stomach clenched, getting so far away from Mac. I pushed it away. She needed me to figure this out, not to coddle her. She had Jarret for that. And Rainer was home now. He might not seem like the type to do that, but he was. Even Anton would when he returned. My job was to fix what was wrong. It always had been.

I drove down the small country road that led to my business office. To people not in the know, it would look like it was just a road that someone had to drive down to get to the tour. They didn't know the amount of time I spent with so-called experts working on this approach over the years. It was all about what they called branding. When the customers turned down this road, they had to feel like they were about to venture into something very special.

The real 'swamp' experience.

We could have, and maybe should have, paved this road. Certainly, the buses would have preferred it not to bounce through the small holes. But what we'd gained in setting the scene this way seemed to have worked.

Not that I thought the whole thing rested on the fucking road. It didn't. We gave a great tour. All of my guides were boat captains and getting various upper level degrees at

LSU in science and history things. They were all a lot smarter than me.

That worked fine. This was just the kind of job they wanted. It was part time, they could manage their hours, make money while they studied. None of them remarked if they found me at all odd.

The place was empty now. Wednesdays, we didn't open until noon. It was the perfect time for me to get in and out without being noticed. I didn't want to answer questions about where I was yet. The business should basically run itself, even if I liked to micromanage.

My office was locked, which made me enormously happy. No one was breaking in during my extended absence.

Not to mention, there was still plenty of evidence that it was running smoothly.

I stopped where I stood. I'd never gotten Mac inside of my offices or on the boats. She'd never been further than my parking lot. In the time we'd hidden her away, it had seemed unsafe. Knowing what I did now, I should have brought her. She'd have liked to have seen this place. Maybe I could have taken one of the airboat tours with her. It had been a long time since I'd done one. I'd love to see it the first time through her eyes.

I unlocked my office and headed for the desk. Another lock had to be opened to get to the phone. I might have been paranoid, but it turned out I was right. The whole world was trying to fuck with my life. I scanned through the phone, looking for the number. Totally not letting myself think about the fact that I could have just googled the guy from home to get the number, since denial was my new best friend, I smelled the wolf.

Stopping what I was doing, I set down my phone. "All

right. Who the fuck is out there?" I gripped the side of my desk. "You don't want to fuck with me right now. I'll tear you in two."

Did I expect a Loup to stumble into my office half formed, looking like the monster it was? No, I didn't. But there it was.

I clenched my teeth. "Boy, did you pick the wrong fucking day to do this."

"Help," its voice grumbled. It was sort of hard to hear it, and if I hadn't spent enough time around these guys to know that they spoke, it would just sound like mishmash to me. But the sonofabitch who was in my place of business was asking for help.

I looked up at the sky, trying to find my equilibrium. Was this for real? Finally, I spoke to him. "I'm not the Omega. This is a place humans go."

He sniffed the air. "Smell her."

Oh, that made sense. I guessed. "I smell like her." I let out a breath I held. "Okay. Here's the deal. The Omega is out of commission at the moment. And you obviously have a really lousy sense of smell. Shouldn't you be...tough or something?"

This was the worst Loup I'd ever encountered. Not that I'd had that many of them. More than I'd ever envisioned having, but whatever. This was Mac's life, and I was happy just to be a part of it. Loving her was everything.

I waved my hand at the Loup. "We can't help you right now."

It stood there and stared at me. Fuck my life. I took a deep breath. "We can't stay here." That much was clear. My wolf prowled on the edges of my consciousness, begging to come out, desperate to shift and kill this abomination. But that wasn't what he was. My human mind could think through this. He wasn't wrong, he was sick. Omegas fixed Loups. My love would not want me to just kill it...ah...him. I took a deep breath.

I nodded toward him. "Come with me."

He tilted his head. What did he understand in that head of his? How often did he stay like a human, and how much like this? I had a million questions, but right now, I had to get him out of this office before someone I worked with showed up and saw him. Then the reports of werewolves would start to appear here, and we could see them on the internet the next time we searched. Or worse, hunters not affiliated with Morgan would...

I stared at him. Morgan was so strong psychically because he was an Alpha as a Loup.

"Tell me something, buddy. Do you ever hear voices?"

I didn't expect him to be able to answer, and he didn't. I wouldn't be able to reach him like this, but my brother Jarret, the oddball we always sort of misunderstood, had been able to connect to Mac psychically. Was that just something he could do? We were going to find out.

"Come on." I pulled on the Loup. He was coming with me.

We both stumbled. He at my unexpected movement, and me because he was a lot heavier than I'd anticipated. I really hoped I wasn't going to have to knock him out and swing him over my shoulder, because as strong as I was, I wasn't at all certain I could actually do that.

He growled, and I responded, letting my wolf come into my voice box. I was tougher than he was. Better he understand that now.

MacKenzie

"I took your memories as a courtesy to you, and this is how you repay me? Using language like that?"

I rolled my eyes. Whoever this guy was, he had no idea just how foul my language could get. Crap was a problem? Maybe I should go ahead and tell him to fuck himself.

"What century were you born in? This is how people talk now. Get over yourself." I looked away from him. I wasn't going to be held hostage by some ambiguous set of rules I was pretty sure he was making up as he went along.

He growled, which was a strange noise. Who growled? I opened my mouth to ask him that, when suddenly, my head wanted to explode. I grabbed on to it, pain rocking me forward, until I almost fell into the water. What in the ever-loving hell was going on? Ouch. Fuck me. Fuck. Fuck. Fuck.

Yes, I was going to use that word just as much as I wanted to, because fuck me, this hurt.

But as it passed, I knew. I was MacKenzie Harper. Mate to Rainer, Preston, Jarret, and Anton. The only Omega born in a generation because of the man standing in front of me. He'd trapped me here with him.

I held my head. Having my memories back wasn't making this better. If anything, it was making it worse. Not that I'd tell Ross how I felt—yes, that was this sonofabitch's name, I remembered it now. He was in control of this situation, and the only thing I could do was try to reason with him so that I could get out of it.

This dock wasn't real. The setting was something he projected into my head. To the best of my recollection, I was home, in the house that was falling down around us, in the swamp. My guys were with me. I'd rescued them. In fact, I'd saved everyone in need who had crossed my path. It had nearly killed me to do so.

Whatever this was, it was what Ross did. He stole people psychically. The strongest Loup ever, or some crap, was now fucking around with me.

"Why did you do this?"

He growled. "Because you shouldn't exist, and I'm trying to understand you."

I sighed. "I'm not really in the mood to go over the nature of existence with you. Why do any of us exist? Why are any of us here? What's the point of life? Blah. Blah. Blah. No."

He pointed at me. "You know that's not what I meant. I prevented Omegas from existing."

I took a deep breath. Yes, I knew exactly what he meant. "How did you do that?"

"It's not hard actually. When we are born, we connect psychically to our pack through the Alpha. It's a simple matter of not letting the Omega connection take place."

I didn't understand any of that. "Is that an Alpha thing? The ability to feel that connection?"

"It is." He sighed like he was bored. "Like you connect. Don't expect to understand it. You're not an Alpha. I don't presume to know how it feels to be an Omega."

Well, that was something. He was sounding...reasonable. "An Alpha who became a Loup. Is that it?"

"Yes. It happens. I know people think that it doesn't, but an Alpha can get lost, even as they run a pack. An Alpha can get lost to the madness."

Yes, but an Alpha should have had a pack to notice. An Alpha should have had someone summon an Omega if they didn't have one in the pack. An Alpha shouldn't have been able to run amok like this without someone getting him some help before it happened.

Why and how did this take place?

I didn't have an Omega I could ask. Of course it would be really helpful to see the old woman from my dreams—who may or may not have been a dead Omega—talking to me right now. Not that I thought that might happen. Ross was clearly controlling my mind.

"What is the plan here? Trap me in here with you indefinitely until I perish? Seems a little beneath you." I knew I should have been controlling my temper, but so far, I wasn't having any luck with it. My fingers tingled. I was going to explode with anger. What would the guys tell me to do? They weren't real breathe-and-relax people. We were werewolves, and this was bullshit.

Ross' eyes flared. "Do you actually think you can win here? Do you actually think that you could beat me in some kind of fight in a world that I am literally controlling?"

I guessed I hadn't done a wonderful job of hiding my feelings. Or maybe he could smell it. I didn't seem to have any of my wolf senses, but that didn't mean that he didn't have some. I stood, staring him in the eyes as best I could, despite the fact that he was significantly taller than me. "You're a Loup. I could help you with that, but I don't think I'm going to because you're an asshole. And I think it might be better for the world that you die. I don't care how rich you are. How powerful you've made yourself. You're clearly just an Alpha whose pack didn't care about him enough to keep him alive."

He growled, this time, a true wolf sound. Yeah...he had some werewolf ability. "How dare you speak to me like that? I could drown you in the lake."

Could he? I supposed it was time to find out. I shoved

him, just as hard as I could. His eyes widened. He hadn't expected that. I did it again while he was surprised, and this time, he stumbled backwards.

Straight into the water.

Never had the sound of a splash ever felt so good.

———

Jarret

"You want me to do what with this Loup?" I stared at the scene in front of me. My brother Preston was holding a Loup's hand on our front porch as though the man was a small child he was worried was about to dart into traffic.

Preston's annoyance was an acrid smell that made me want to gag. When Pres got upset, he really ran with the emotion, and maybe it was the little brother in me that never wanted to make him mad, but I always wanted to do anything to not turn his annoyance into anger. I was bigger than him when we were werewolves, but he was meaner than me, hands down.

Still, I wasn't going to be bullied into... I wasn't sure what he wanted me to do with that sick man he should not have brought anywhere near the house where our sick mate suffered upstairs.

"I want you to get in his head, use the psychic link Morgan has over all Loups, follow it, and break the link to Mac."

Yeah...that's what he said when he arrived. I looked at Miranda, and then Rainer, to see if either of them followed what he said any better than I did, but both were silent. They were pissed at each other. I could smell that, too.

Sometimes, my nose was a real burden. Humans didn't know how lucky they had it.

"How am I going to do that?" I rubbed the back of my neck. I'd do whatever Kenzie needed, but it really sounded like Preston might have lost his mind.

He waved his hand in the air. "You just mind melded with Mac. Do that again."

Oh, that was where he'd gotten the idea. "Mind melded? Like Spock? From *Star Trek*?"

"Sure. Whatever. I didn't watch the show. Pointy ears. That's what I remember from just fandom stuff."

I did watch the show. A lot. I loved it. But I was going to leave this alone, because arguing with Pres when he was like this was like hitting my head against a brick wall repeatedly. "Preston—"

"Hold on," Rainer interrupted. "This is a really good idea."

Preston nodded fast. "See? I knew it was."

"No doubt, it's a wonderful idea," I agreed. "Problem is, I don't know how to do that. I don't think it was me who made that happen, per se. It was Kenzie. Our Omega mate, who is amazing. She did it. I went along for the ride." Rainer rocked back on his feet. His thinking pose. Uh-oh. No. "Rainer?"

He held my gaze, and I couldn't look away. "Here's the thing...I think you can do this."

"Have you all lost it?" Where was Anton? He was reasonable. He'd at least be able to see they'd gone off the deep end. Why not ask me to shift into an alligator? I'd probably sooner be able to do that than this.

Rainer took a step toward me. "Listen...one of the last coherent things that our mate knew was that she had lost her Omega powers. They were gone. Stolen by the piece of shit who's doing this to all of us."

I waited, but he didn't continue. "And?"

"If she has lost her powers, then she didn't draw you into where she was. No way could MacKenzie do that. Not if she's powerless."

I walked to the window. "Maybe she only thinks she's powerless."

"I think I'm going to trust our mate to know if she has her Omega abilities or not." Rainer snorted. "And spare you her wrath by not telling her that you suggested she didn't know herself."

I rubbed my arms. "Rainer, you know that's not what I'm doing."

"No, what you're doing is negating the idea that you have the ability to do this. I get it. Not a traditional wolf power. But it's yours. And there is lots of precedent for it. This is a threat. You're a high up beta in my pack. You could be Alpha if I weren't here."

I snorted. "I could never be Alpha."

"You could, but that isn't for me to tell you. Besides, I don't need you to get all growly and challenge me right now. Do it later. Fuck. He's a threat. You can help eliminate that threat. That's what enforcers do. That's how pack works. We all have gifts. They come from our wolves. Yours might be able to connect to other wolves differently. I am asking you to use it."

I ran a hand through my hair. "What was it that Gus used to call me? Problematic. That's always what I am, right? Even as a wolf, I have to be an oddball."

Rainer put his hand on my shoulder. I didn't know why, but the touch helped. Maybe that was a wolf thing, too. Just because I could now shift didn't mean that I understood everything that came with it. We should all have had pack instruction as children, and instead, we'd been too busy suppressing our very instincts because of this fuckin' Loup who now had my girl.

"Gus doesn't have a way with words. Whatever he meant by that, I am grateful for whatever you can do. Okay? I don't find it odd. I mean...Anton wrote books with hidden clues in them. None of us are exactly normal, right? But I know that in the past, there were things that everyone could do. That's what makes us unique. That's what I need from you. What makes you, you." He paused. "That's what MacKenzie needs."

I rolled my eyes at him. "That's dirty pool right there, Rainer. Using her at the end like this to get me to agree. Fine. Yes, I'll try. But I don't know how I'm going to do it. I held Kenzie and sort of pleaded with her to let me in."

Preston grinned. "Well, come give big boy here a hug. Let's see if that works."

Fuck my life.

CHAPTER 4
RAINER

I knew I was asking a lot of Jarret. Sure, little brother, go ahead and make a psychic connection with the Loup. No big deal. Just get right on that. How was he supposed to do that? I had a houseful of older werewolves, and there wasn't one—including Miranda, who stared at the three of us with the Loup like we'd all grown a second head —that I'd trust to instruct me on anything.

Why? Well, the problem was two-fold. First, the ones who signed the Accord and forced us into submission had all become weak in my eyes. Even my own parents. We never should have been in this situation. How was I to lead? Well, I certainly couldn't learn that from my parents. My biological father was gone now, and much as I loved Kevin, and would mourn him every day for the rest of my life, he'd been pivotal in the Accords, so sad about Anton being taken, he'd led us straight into self-destruction and not even seen it.

We were all of us flawed. I didn't expect perfection from any living creature. But they had fucked this up big time, and now it was my woman and my family who had to fix this somehow.

"Can I speak to you?" It was Miranda.

I shook my head. "No."

I didn't need wolf senses to know that pissed her off. She was strong, but I'd discovered I was stronger. She was in my house. Here, she would do as I wanted, and I didn't wish to hear from her right now. My heart was too angry. I wouldn't say or do anything productive, and she had nothing to teach me right now. Miranda had opted not to have her pack sign the Accords. I'd give her credit for that, but her Omega had died. Mine was not going to do that. She didn't know how to save MacKenzie any more than I did. In fact, she probably knew less. She'd *let* her sister die.

She stormed from the room.

"If you're not careful, she's going to take her pack and go home." Preston raised his eyebrows, the Loup he held not seeming to follow our conversation as he stared dazedly at all of us.

I shook my head. "She won't. She's fascinated with this, and we have the only living Omega. She's going to need MacKenzie for her pack. If she takes off now, she's screwing herself."

"You seem...frustrated with her," Jarret supplied.

Now was not the time for me to lose my temper with them, too. "I am. Frustrated is not the right word. I find her presence to be jarring and disconcerting. And... I don't want to discuss this right now." I nodded toward the Loup. "Jarret, your turn."

I didn't need them to tell me that it was hard for two Alphas to be in the same room together. I was fully aware. Unlike them, I could remember a lot about pack before our parents and their generation fucked it up. Cristian never liked to leave the house more than he had to, lest he accidentally run into another Alpha. And he had followed Kevin's lead as their true Alpha. So it was very complicated and bound to get worse for my brothers soon, as their natural Alpha abilities were all showing up. One of them might very well challenge me, and I might let them have it if it meant I could love on MacKenzie all day.

But I didn't have time to become a shut-in right then. And this was my house, so if anyone was going to be uncomfortable here, it could be Miranda, not me.

My second youngest brother approached the Loup. A muscle ticked in his jaw. "Really? I have to hug him?"

"I won't let him hurt you. He's actually pretty...docile." Preston looked between the Loup and Jarret.

Jarret growled, a strange sound from him. He was the gentlest of us all. People might think that was Anton, but it absolutely was not. The silence lent itself to that impression, but it was wrong. Jarret was the least likely to get angry or violent.

When he spoke, it was through gritted teeth. "I'm not afraid. I just don't go around hugging people. Not regularly, okay?"

I didn't blame him. I wouldn't want to hug the Loup either. "Maybe just put your hand on him or something."

He shot me a look that spoke of pain later. I almost smiled. I'd take what he dished out, gladly, if this worked.

Jarret put his arms around the Loup. He winced like it pained him, and I was sure it did, from the smell alone. That man needed a bath, and he needed one yesterday.

I wasn't volunteering for the job.

"Nothing's happening." Jarret stated the obvious.

Yes, okay, that was true. "Are you trying?"

"I told you that I don't have a clue how I did that earlier. It's not like a skill I have. Paint walls, inserts oneself into a..."

He stopped talking, and suddenly, my brother wasn't there anymore. He was present in body only. The Loup's eyes closed, and it was everything I could do to not rush forward and rip Jarret backward. That was my little brother. I'd pulled him out of the swamp once when he'd almost drowned. It was hard to not do the same right here. Of course, it was like I'd pushed him into the water this time.

Preston met my gaze. "It's okay."

I hoped he was right and concerned he'd read me so well. It was the scent thing these days. I had to get used to it, again. Too many years not smelling anything of significance from forcing our bodies to pretend to be human, and I was out of practice with how to deal with everyone smelling every emotion I had. Of course, Pres was out of the habit of minding his own fucking business and not commenting on everything he could smell.

Jarret gasped and fell backwards. I darted forward and managed to catch him in time so he didn't hit the ground

"Jarret?" Even a human would hear the sound of my concern at this moment. My little brother had just collapsed. "Speak to me."

He rubbed his face and then laughed. Shit. What had happened? He didn't smell like a Loup, but had I just infected him with some kind of madness?

"That was...awful." Jarret shuddered and then pulled out of my arms. "I could see a lot of this guy's memories. He had a whole life. He was an electrician. Couldn't handle The Accords. It was hard to get through just being stuck with him."

I sighed. So I'd put him through that, and it hadn't

worked. "Sorry it was a waste of your abilities, but at least we know you can do it."

He shook his head. "You misunderstand me. I didn't finish. I got through. I found him."

A car screeched to a stop, and annoyance flooded me. What now? I was about to get incredible information, and of course, someone was here to fuck that up. Anton ran from the car. I looked down at my phone. Wow. He must have driven at a breakneck speed. I'd give him shit about it later.

That should have taken six hours, but it took five. Crazy man. Not that I could blame him for wanting to do this fast.

I turned back around to Jarret. "Go on then. What happened?"

"He's not close. Like a long-distance pull. Hard to explain. I followed and followed it, and then landed right in front of him. I don't think he knew it was me."

That was good, but I still didn't know exactly where we needed to go. "Jarret? Focus."

"Sorry, my head isn't clear. He's in the Pacific Northwest."

Just then, Anton burst through the screen door. He held up his notebook. I was glad to see him. Things went better when we were all together. They just did, always. We'd always worked better as a team. "Pacific Northwest. Jarret was able to find him. Was there a lake?"

Preston rushed past us and into the house. I wasn't sure where he was going, but I didn't care. Jarret was so close to giving us the answers we needed. He scrunched up his face. "I didn't see a lake. Just Ross sitting in a chair. Log cabin walls, like that's what they looked like. Hard to explain."

That didn't give me a lot to work with. The Pacific Northwest was a fairly substantial space to deal with. It wasn't like we could just go running around the whole area until we stumbled upon a werewolf named Ross.

Anton held up his notebook and placed it really close to my face. Too close, in fact, for me to be able to read, but that was fine. I backed it up. "I get it. You want me to look at this now." What had he found?

Right there in front of me, now that I could see it, were the words 'Goose Lake.' I blinked. "Where is this? Goose Lake? Where is it located?"

Because if it was somewhere in Texas, that wasn't going to be particularly helpful to me. Not now that Jarret had found the Pacific Northwest, and what was I going to do if they contradicted each other? Who was right?

Anton held up his phone. It had the same app that had been on the tablet and let him speak with it. Even though he preferred not to most of the time. I didn't blame him. He could make himself understood perfectly well without the interference a good portion of the time. But now he was using the app. He must really want me to understand.

"Oregon."

I smiled, satisfaction rushing through me for the first time in a long while. Now we were getting somewhere. "Bingo."

Preston ran back. He held his laptop. "Give me the details."

"Goose Lake. Oregon." I looked at Jarret. "How did you know so specifically?"

He lay back on the ground, sprawled out like he intended to stay there permanently. "There's a sign. I'm going to sleep now."

I grinned. "No, not there, brother." Preston went over and picked him up one-armed, swinging him over his shoulder. I shook my head. Sometimes, they were ridiculous. It was a good thing I loved them so much. "Put him on the couch."

I didn't know exactly how old the couch we kept on the porch was, but it held Jarret up when Preston set him down on it. Anton grinned at both of them. Yes, we worked in this way. We always had, even when we had been so full of angst, we'd been taking it out on each other. This part of us worked.

Still with one arm holding his laptop, Preston swung around and used his now free other hand to start typing. "Yep. It's one of them. There are werewolf sightings there. Quite a few. Our boy is not that careful."

"Great."

Now we had somewhere to go, and I was one step closer to killing that son of a bitch.

_____

MacKenzie

He was wet, and he had no idea what to do about it. I tilted my head. "You could end this farce and go dry off."

Ross growled as he pulled himself out of the water. "How did you do that?"

"I'm talented and amazing. Like a unicorn. I'm the Omega that shouldn't be. I can do all sorts of things that I shouldn't be able to do."

Truth was that I had no idea whatsoever how I had done that. I'd wanted him to fall, so I'd shoved. It was that easy. Push. Boom. Wet. I sighed. This was going to be a long encounter with Ross. He'd been doing this forever, had so many powers I couldn't fathom them, and he was sick in the head. I wasn't a psychologist. Hell, I wasn't even a college graduate.

I wouldn't even say that I was one of those people who

really understood others' motivations all the time. I knew there were some folks like that, but I wasn't one of them. I'd been too far removed hiding the fact that I really wanted to live my truth as a werewolf to really get to know anyone outside of my family.

But I was the Omega, and it was my job to take care of werewolves who needed me. Sometimes that was emotionally. Certainly, my loves carried wounds that I helped them with. But I would suffer in pain the rest of my life before I gave this man an ounce of my time making him feel better.

No, some people had to die, and he was one of them. My mouth watered. I was a strong, tough werewolf, and I'd take him down. I didn't always have to be gentle and kind. In fact, it went against my nature.

"You want to kill me."

I wouldn't deny it. "You're a selfish, narcissistic person. I don't know why the Omegas didn't help you. I might even feel sorry for you, if you hadn't turned around and done what you did. Killed everyone. Kept them from being born because your wolf is strong despite the madness. The Loups who come to me for help, I feel sorry for them. But they are actively trying to get better. You're just pathetic and unkind."

He surged forward. "You don't know my story."

"I don't have to. The boo hoo woe is me routine you want to do right now will never and I mean *ever* make up for the genocide you've done to the Omegas. The way you have ruined every werewolf alive. Destroyed families. Wrecked lives. I don't care why you did it. The only solution for someone like you is death."

He grabbed my arms. His breath stunk, which was saying a lot, since we were in some kind of confine he'd created. The wetness of his hand seeped into my arms through my clothes. "You will fix me if I tell you to."

I tipped up my chin. "Not in a million fucking years."

Anton

I'd never seen a group of so many people get ready so fast all at once. Cars were packed, and everyone was quickly where they needed to be to go save MacKenzie, which included bringing her with us. Everyone wanted her safe because she was the Omega. Not the four of us. I could say beyond a shadow of a doubt—not that I ever said anything—that my brothers wanted her back because they loved her as I did.

Screw the Omega thing.

I strode toward the motorhome we had gotten at some point—I wasn't sure when or how, because I'd been out of it —and rushed on board before I was left behind. It wasn't that anyone would mean to forget me, but I'd realized very early on as a child that since I couldn't holler out *hey wait* when people got moving, that I'd better make sure I was one of the first people to get in a vehicle at any time, lest they leave without me.

I didn't let myself think about those times very much. It was better not to dwell on things that I couldn't control. Besides, things were getting better. Massively. And it was all thanks to the fact that MacKenzie lived in the world. How had I not known that? It seemed like the moment she breathed air, I should have somehow known.

The whole universe should have slowed its spin so everyone on the planet knew the most wonderful person who'd ever existed had finally arrived.

I sat down on a couch in the vehicle and waited. Her brother Isaac was going to drive, and it looked like Preston was going to sit shotgun next to him. They must have some sort of routine in this, because they looked comfortable in the way that only came from experience.

I'd spent my life watching my family. Analyzing them. Seeing what made them tick. I loved them and would kill for them in a second. It made me nuts when I lost time with them, which was why I couldn't lose Preston for all of those years when he took himself off to the swamp, leaving the rest of us behind. He was having memories and experiences I knew nothing about.

He'd changed, and I hadn't been there to watch it, to understand how that worked and why.

And then I'd come back, and we'd all gotten to fall in love with the same girl and have her love us back. Such a gift. Frankly, a miracle, and I didn't believe in such things. And now they'd had a whole bunch more things happen while I'd been trapped in my mind and unable to help.

Rainer sat down across from me. Although he looked calm, the acrid scent hitting my nose told me that my oldest brother was filled with stress and anxiety. I was as well, and I must scent the same to him. Better to not mention it.

"You okay?" He lifted his gaze to meet mine, and I nodded. I wasn't, but sometimes you just lied, because what was the other person going to do if you weren't? It wasn't as though Rainer could snap his fucking fingers and she'd magically appear fine and at home where we could all live happily ever after. That wasn't going to be how our lives worked.

Rainer shut his eyes and leaned against the couch. He wasn't going to sleep. He was going to wait. I wished I could do that. Just sit with my eyes closed and stay silent until I had somewhere to go.

"Rainer." Miranda stormed into the motorhome

followed by Jarret, who carried our love. He didn't comment, just nodding at me as he carried her to the back of the vehicle. There was a small bedroom there, and when he didn't return, I presumed he'd lain down with her.

My oldest brother opened his eyes. If he could dish out death in that moment, he would. I knew the look well. Mostly Preston had been on the other end of that glare when we'd been kids, but there it was just the same.

Isaac pulled the RV out, and our journey began, the other Alpha was with us whether Rainer liked it or not. Of course, he could demand we stop and put her out on the side of the road. But he was a Southern man, and our mother, for all her flaws, had taught us better than that. He wasn't going to put a woman out on the road.

Banging hit the side of the motorhome, and we all turned. She sighed. "Stop, please. It's one of my mates."

I should have known. I'd never have let my mate go without one of us, too. Isaac sighed but stopped. He opened the door, and the tallest of Miranda's men strode on. He was out of breath. Her guys tended to be silent, but unlike me, they actually could speak and didn't. Maybe that was a quality she looked for in a mate. Silent and deadly.

He shot his mate a look and strode to the back, where he could watch her but not overwhelm her. I'd do the same for MacKenzie if she were here and needed it, except I might sit right next to her, since I wasn't sure I could be separated from her ever again. I might have to live glued to her side.

She made my heart beat. She made my blood flow. She made it so I could breathe. MacKenzie Harper was my entire world, and I loved her completely. What was amazing was that she loved me like that, too. Understood me, somehow.

MacKenzie was my heart.

My hands itched. I wanted to write, but I didn't have my laptop, So I ignored the inclination.

"You have to listen to me."

Rainer stared at Miranda. I shifted in my seat. Were we going to fight her? Yes, she was an Alpha, but she was also a woman. I'd never fought a female. Still, I'd have Rainer's back, now and always. Otherwise, I'd be going into the bedroom and lying down with Jarret and MacKenzie.

My oldest brother tilted his head. "Okay. Talk. Since you've busted your way on here."

She ignored his jibe, which was impressive because he probably deserved to get called out on that. "You can't be Alpha of everyone. Yes, this is your battle. I am the one who insisted on it. But, Rainer, I see how they're all starting to fawn around you. They think you're going to be their Alpha. You can't be. The Omega's mates just have to concentrate on her."

I leaned forward. What did she think we were doing?

A spike of amusement hit me from Rainer. He thought this was funny?

"You know what I'm sick of?" He ran a hand over his chin. This was the most unshaved I'd ever seen Rainer. I touched my own cheeks. Come to think of it, I also hadn't shaved. We were all going to be going for the bearded look soon.

I didn't know what he was sick of, but I was excited to hear it. There were about a million things I was sick of.

Miranda sighed. "What's that?"

"People telling us what we should and shouldn't do. As far as I'm concerned, the way it was done before was wrong. Maybe if the Omegas hadn't been so isolated, so completely consumed by just their own mates, then everyone could have noticed when things started to go badly for them.

Maybe their mates could have gotten them help earlier and they wouldn't have died." All of his amusement was gone. My wolf prowled to the surface. This wasn't an ideal place to have a fight, but I was up for it if that was what was going to happen.

Miranda's mate growled, and I shot him a look. I could take him. Funny how I knew that. It was like even though my wolf wasn't currently shifted or dominant, he knew instinctively who we were capable of handling. I was a lot stronger than most people realized, and that suited me fine. Let them underestimate me to their own peril.

Rainer held up his hand. "We're just talking here."

Miranda breathed hard. "I assure you, we weren't ignoring the Omegas. My sister was one of them."

"Yes, I know. And now my mate has to fight this battle for all of them. If everyone wants to follow me, they can. I won't turn anyone away, but neither am I seeking this. If I'm Alpha, so be it." He nodded toward me. "He'd be better at this than I am."

Oh fuck that, Rainer wasn't dragging me into this mess. I wasn't going to be anyone's Alpha. Nope. My wolf agreed. We'd kick ass and take names, but we weren't going to make decisions about pack lands and food supplies. No, absolutely not.

"So you won't step away."

Rainer tilted his head. "Don't be afraid. I don't want your pack, Miranda. When this is over, take your people and go back home. If they'll still have you. But maybe it isn't me they want so much as the swamp. It's hard to be there and not know that you're home."

And that was the complete truth.

CHAPTER 5

MACKENZIE

He came at me like he meant to kill me, and I believed that he would. Had he done this before? How many had he done this to? Had he taken over the brains of every Omega in the world and tortured them on this dock until they were dead? I wasn't going out like that. But some things were different for me. Maybe because I knew who he was and what he was doing.

One of my teachers had told me when I was young that knowledge was power. In my case, I would assume that remained true.

Another thought dawned on me just as fast. Maybe it was just that my wolf was really powerful. I'd managed to become an Omega when there had been no chance of that happening. Didn't that mean I had to be strong?

I shook my head. It was weird to think nice things about myself. I'd been so beaten down for such a long time. And that was because of this man in front of me.

"How am I here? How did I manage to squeeze in as an Omega when you had it so locked down? I guess I'm stronger than you are. Asshole."

It felt good to hurl that word at him. Sure, I should have been above such things, and maybe in a better time, when I could meditate three times a day, I'd manage to find my better self and feel awful about how low I'd gone here. But right now? It felt fucking good.

"Asshole." This time, I shouted it.

He lunged at me, shifting as he did. I paused to stare at him. Ross was a Loup, through and through. He might seem to make sense sometimes, but he was absolutely not okay in the head. Looking like a werewolf who was trying to walk on two feet, he was like something out of a bad monster movie. I tilted my head. I'd seen a ton of Loups in the brief time I'd been living like this. There was nothing special about him. Like this? He was just a run of the mill Loup that wasn't that interesting to me.

I steeled my spine. Fine. If he wanted to play, that was what we would do. I shifted into my wolf form. Most of the time, this drove Rainer crazy. He didn't want me in the fray of fighting if I could get hurt. It was his job to protect me. I was too unique in this world to be risked. I had a hard time listening to him, because my natural instinct was to help, to fight back. Maybe it came from having all those older brothers.

I didn't know, and I didn't suppose it mattered.

I wasn't fixing this Loup so he could be absolved of his sins by some excuse that he had been crazy. He was going to be eliminated, and maybe this was pointless since I was in his fake environment. I probably couldn't hurt him. But boy, could I make it hurt.

I growled and lunged at him. This would be so nice if I had Rainer, Preston, Jarret, and Anton with me. It must have been a wolf thing, but I loved being with them in a fight. They were my pack.

MacKenzie...

I jolted and moved out of the way of Ross' attack. Loups were easy to get away from, at least for me. It might be an Omega thing, but I found them very easy to dart and maneuver against. But I'd heard Anton, and it almost threw me off my game.

Funny. I'd only heard him once when we were connected in his mind during the time I'd freed him from Ross' clutches. But I was hearing him now. Was he able to do the same for me?

Anton...

I heard him gasp. *You can hear me?*

I always could. Our hearts were connected. I'd be able to understand all of them if they needed me to, but it had just been incredibly easy with Anton. I'd just known what he wanted to say, and he'd hardly had to use the tablet at all to communicate with me. We'd just connected.

And now I could hear him. Was that possible?

MacKenzie...

There he was again.

Can you hear me?

I could, but I had no way of telling him that. None at all. It was like an echo of a sound. A second later, Jarret appeared before me. He was there, and a second later, he wasn't. I swung around, growling, but not at Ross. It was frustration. The Loup could go drown in the lake. I didn't care right then. Because I wanted to be with my guys, and maybe I was having a Dorothy moment, but there was no place like home.

I wanted to see their faces, touch their hands, hear their voices. I needed these men. They were my home, my loves, and my pack. And I was sick of being trapped by this egocentric Loup who couldn't decide if he did or didn't want to be saved. That was fine. I'd answer the question for him. I wasn't going to do it.

Like a lasso, I sent my consciousness toward Anton as though I might latch on to him and pull myself free from here. Somehow, it worked. I floated. It was a funny feeling, one I couldn't have imagined, but it was like I was leaving my body. Although I supposed it was the opposite problem. I was actually going to my body, not away from it.

It was like a yank, and I was there. I opened my eyes, and all four of my guys stared down at me. I groaned. "How long was I in there?"

"Days," Rainer answered. He patted Anton and then Jarret on the back. "Good work you two. Sweetheart, I...I'm not sure I can express to you... I..." He struggled until he finally found his words. "It's so good to see you looking at us, MacKenzie."

His gaze spoke of adoration, of a million things he hadn't been able to say right then.

It was so good to see them. I looked around, trying to get my bearings. "Are we in the motorhome?"

Preston nodded. "We're on the move. Don't worry, Mac. We've got this. And you're here. How?"

I stared at Anton and Jarret. "It was like I attached to them and pulled out."

"That's great." Jarret knelt down next to the bed. "Can you stay this way, or could he take you back?"

The truth was that I didn't know the answer to that. This was all new to me. I'd never fathomed being in this situation, and I hadn't a clue how to proceed forward. Plus, there were no Omegas around to guide me, if they even knew how, which I doubted. Every day was something new; every minute, I had to guess what to do next.

But these guys were here with me. I took Preston and

Jarret's hands, since they were the closest. Anton's gaze held my own as though we were magnetically connected, never to separate again. Rainer was a solid anchor. He was there for me in a way that told me he'd shoulder my problems every day of his life. My job was to see to it that he didn't have to do that.

I blinked. I couldn't afford to get lost in my love for them right now. It would be easy, just to float away in my feelings. But I needed answers and to give them some.

"I don't know." I sat up straighter so I wasn't lying flat. "Are we alone? Who is driving?"

Jarret squeezed our hands together. "Isaac. And Miranda plus her mate Groucho are here."

I blinked. "Groucho?"

"I can't remember his name. I'm just going to call him Groucho. I like it."

Preston laughed, throwing his head back. "I think I'm rubbing off on you, Jarret."

"MacKenzie?" Rainer brought my attention back to the here and now. "Tell me what happened."

So I did. How I had found myself on that dock with no explanation on how I'd gotten there, with no memory, how he'd given it back to me. Then he wanted to be fixed, even though he'd said he didn't. All of it. The whole time there, and how bizarre it really had been.

"The thing was, he doesn't even know what he wants. He's out there yelling he doesn't need to be fixed, that he just wants to punish and kill Omegas, but when I deny him the service of the Omega, he gets mad."

Rainer ran a hand through his hair. He wasn't wearing it in the usual man-bun. It was down around his shoulders. "He's able to do the connections because he's an Alpha. Living an obscenely long life. Maybe that's because of the

Loup thing. I don't know. I wish I understood more of how this worked. But truthfully, I don't. Loups were to be disposed of when I was a kid. I don't remember there being a whole lot of discussion about helping back then, but then the Omegas were outside of pack influence, too. Maybe our Omegas were out there helping people and I just had no idea. Maybe it was like a Loup either got killed by pack enforcers or helped by the Omega. I never gave it any damn thought."

What he said was interesting to me. I chewed on my lip. "He can connect as the Alpha. Could you? To keep me here? Could you hold on to my wolf and not let him draw me in again so that I'm taken over?"

I didn't want to be back on that dock with Ross. I didn't mind the Loups coming to me. They woke me up, interfered in my life, and were otherwise disruptive, but that was my job. Whether I asked for this or not, I needed to care for them. But Ross was different. Those men who showed up at my door were pitiful in the sense that they made my heart ache for their situations. Ross did not. Maybe once he would have, but what he had done went beyond the bounds of acceptability on any scale. I could not—would not—put up with this. He was to be eliminated.

End of story.

Rainer nodded. "I could try. I'm not entirely certain how to do that." A muscle ticked in his jaw. "But I suppose I could ask our...guest if she knows how to do that. If anyone would know, she would."

I smirked. There was clearly no love lost between Rainer and Miranda. I liked her just fine, but it was bound to be different with the two of them. And there was something about Rainer getting a little growly that really appealed to my wolf side. It was as though I didn't mind him being rough and difficult. That was how he was supposed to be.

It showed me the world hadn't broken him, not even when they'd locked him away. I smiled. Somehow, I knew that his wolf was too strong for that.

That was true for all of them. Preston, with his easy smile and laughter, hid away his pain at losing his family, and yet he was able to cope and push through things faster than anyone I knew. Jarret, who doubted himself at every corner, didn't see his own worth, and somehow still managed to pull out an Alpha wolf that was strong and sure of his place in the world. And finally Anton, who had been so abused, it might have destroyed someone with less internal strength. Something he must have cultivated all alone, since the world did nothing to help find that place inside of him.

I loved them all. Deeply.

There was no time like the present to start figuring these things out. I swung my legs over the bed to get up, nearly colliding with Preston when I did. He winked at me before he kissed me hard on the lips. I sighed against him and giggled. Bumping into Preston had its perks.

Pres pulled back, and I was pulled into a kiss with Jarret. He rubbed our noses together before he placed a gentle caress on me, lips to lips.

"Missed you," he whispered in my ear.

I leaned against him. My plans had been to charge from the room, but this was more important. Little moments with them. We had so few, as we were constantly running from one terrible thing to another. In this tiny bedroom in this motorhome I'd illegally bought using Gus' credit card, I was going to take a moment to breathe.

Jarret let me go, and I stepped into Rainer's arms. I

sighed, not in exasperation but in adoration. How did he not know how strong and powerful he was? I loved being his. Finally, Anton drew me to him. He placed my hands over his heart. I smiled. Yes, I loved when he did this. The next second, he placed his own hand over my heart. We stood there for a second, and even though I could anticipate what he was about to do, I loved it just the same. He put his nose right on the spot on my shoulder where he'd marked me.

That had been his spot since the first night we'd met. He'd claimed it and known we were meant to be before I'd even understood what was going on.

"I heard you. In my mind. While I was there." I was speaking in starts and stops, but that was okay. Some occasions didn't need complete thoughts and sentences. This was one of them. I spun around to Jarret. "And I saw you."

Preston put his arms around Jarret and Anton's shoulders. "My little brothers, so talented, and they weren't going to ever be their wolves. Look what the world would have missed out on."

He didn't understand his role. I tilted my head, letting the wolf come into my eyes. I preferred it like this. In fact, if I had a say, I'd spend the majority of my life letting my wolf share my vision. It was so much more natural. "You understand that you are the rope that ties us all together, don't you? We all connected to you. At the end of the day, this wouldn't be without you, Preston."

"Absolutely." Jarret agreed as Anton nodded.

Rainer put his arm around Preston. "She's right."

"Aw, fuck this noise." Pres pulled away. "I don't do sappy-dappy. You guys know that. So thank you, Mac. But I am perfectly fine being the one running the swamp tour that none of you understand."

It was everything I could do not to crack up laughing.

Okay, he wanted to seem mysterious and misunderstood. Fine. We'd let him think he was, when in reality, he was huge-hearted, family-oriented, and he'd only isolated himself because he couldn't stand to watch his family fall apart. We were all together now, and if I had anything to do about it, we always would be. They were my guys, my pack. Everyone else could come and go. We were together. Period.

I didn't push us on, didn't make any of us go do what we had to do. As far as I was concerned, we could stay here all day.

———

Miranda looked like she'd swallowed a bad lemon. "I've never done such a thing."

Well, she was no help. I smiled at her. Miranda had been a huge help to us, and her daughter was mated to my brother Agustin. The motorhome sped fast down the highway as my oldest brother, Isaac, hummed to himself in the driver's seat. This was so strangely normal, it just indicated we'd been doing this too much.

I wanted the swamp. Quiet. And the life we were going to begin to build—minus violence and drama.

"That's okay…"

Rainer held up his hand. "Hold on. You have a huge pack. A bunch of people who are connected to you. Are you sure that you aren't connected to them on some other level? Some way that you can reach them?"

She shifted in her seat. "No. They obey and listen because I'm the strongest wolf. That's how packs work. Your father Kevin was an Alpha before the Accords put them all aside. Was he connected psychically?"

Rainer shook his head. "Well, I'd ask him, but he's dead."

Miranda got to her feet. "You could ask your mother."

"She's grieving another husband. I think she has enough to go through without me bringing this up right now. It's fine if you don't know, Miranda. Perfectly all right. We don't have to make a big thing about this."

She hunched over, her voice going wolf when she spoke to him. "It's not something I can do. It's not something every Alpha can do. Most can't. If that Loup can, then it's very bad, but I am not going to be made to feel..."

Rainer held up his hands, but there was no surrender in his scent. "No one is telling you to feel anything at all."

"Rainer..."

I stepped between them, putting my hands on both of them, one on each of their chests. "Okay, guys, let's take a deep breath and stop this show. What's going on here?" I loved Rainer growly, but this was about to get violent. Miranda's mate was two seconds away from going after Preston while Miranda took on Rainer. Everyone would end up fighting. Isaac wasn't that good of a driver. We'd have an accident, and forget getting to wherever we were going. I still wasn't one hundred percent sure of the location, but I knew I'd rather not end up dead on the road or impaled by Miranda's husband. That seemed simple.

Miranda growled. "Your mate is always baiting me. He won't listen."

"You constantly smell like challenge. I don't need to be instructed by you on how I'm going to live my life, and you don't respect that I know what I'm doing. I'd challenge you to have done better given the circumstances and the entire lack of instruction we received from your generation."

Her eyes went wolf. "I didn't abandon my pack. That was your family."

"I'm not my family. I didn't make their mistakes, and I don't deserve your disdain. I can smell it, and it makes me want to take your fucking head off."

Miranda growled loudly. I was standing in between them, and this might go very badly. I wasn't prepared to stop it. Rainer was my mate. Without question, I'd take his side. But this wasn't an Omega issue. It was an Alpha problem.

And Rainer was my Alpha.

Miranda lowered her eyes. "You're right. I have been holding you responsible for what your parents did."

Rainer was so quiet. Was he going to answer her? Isaac cleared his throat. "Should I pull over?"

I loved my brother, but for now, I ignored him. Finally, Rainer spoke. "They made big, huge mistakes. Unforgivable. They never should have given in to the pressure of the Accords. They abandoned our kind. It was not okay. But I held out until I had no choice because I was framed for murder. I didn't want this."

"I know." She met her mate's gaze and nodded, something unspoken said. "I've been treating you with disrespect. That stops now."

He nodded. "I'm not interested in taking your pack. They're pack. I want my family. The swamp. I want this over. You can and have helped with that when this Loup took me under. I owe you my thanks."

It was like a truce had suddenly been called. The sweet, pleasant scent of peace flooded the vehicle. I took a deep breath.

"So the pulling over?"

Preston shook his head. "No, man. We're fine. I'm

coming up there with you." He winked at me. "Your brother does better when he has someone to talk to."

"You know." Jarret cleared his throat. "You could drive if you were worried about it."

Preston shrugged. "Then what would Isaac do?"

We fell into easiness, all of us sitting down. I leaned on Anton, listening to his heartbeat. Wherever we were going, this wasn't going to be pleasant. Ross hadn't lived this long by being powerless. My stomach growled.

Jarret got to his feet. "I'm going to make you something."

"Thank you, and I should probably shower." Did I smell bad? Even with my wolf senses, it was hard to tell how I scented in particular. I should...

A pain hit my head, and I grabbed on to it. This time I knew exactly what was happening to me. "It's Ross."

Rainer strode to me, bending down to meet me with eye contact. "He's not taking you this time."

"How can you stop it?" I met his gaze and managed to not look down. Sometimes it was easy to not feel submissive to Rainer, sometimes it was much harder. But right now, I needed him. It was a different feeling. Rainer would take care of me. I just knew it.

Why that was... Well, it was a simple answer, and one I realized in just seconds while I held Ross out of my head. He was my Alpha. I'd never had one before him. My family had been out of wolf life for a long time before I was born. I'd had natural feelings of submissiveness when I met Rainer, but it was hard to understand it because my Omega nature fought the traditional roles that were played in pack.

But now? It was easy. I slipped into his care easily. I didn't have to stay here forever. Rainer wouldn't even want me to. He was the first person to say to me that I wasn't submissive as an Omega. That being said, I wasn't Omega in that moment. I was MacKenzie Harper, Rainer's mate, and Rainer was all Alpha.

When I had to be strong, I could be. This wasn't that moment.

"Give him to me," he whispered the words, and just as though I blew him a kiss, I handed Ross over to him.

It was a choice to trust him, to know that when I couldn't be strong, I didn't have to be because he could shoulder it when I couldn't. What was more was that he didn't have to do that alone. Right here in the motorhome, Preston, Jarret, Anton, my brother, and even Miranda and her mate were here to help him. In the same way I could call upon his strength, if he needed to, he could reach for theirs.

How had I not understood what a gift it was to have pack? How had I not grasped the significance of knowing there would always be people who were there to care for you when you couldn't be tough?

And to know that when it was time, he would never expect me to stay submissive. Rainer would absolutely step back and let me be the Omega I needed to be. He loved me so much that he would always be what I needed him to be, just as I would for him.

Right now, I couldn't handle Ross. He had my number and had already proven he could take my mind away from me. But I'd taken Rainer and the others back from him. It was better to let them deal with his manipulations. I could save them. They couldn't save me.

The circular nature of this worked. I'd never stop being grateful.

Rainer smiled. "He left. But check me."

I put my hand on his cheek. We wouldn't be screwed with again. It turned out as a pack, we were much stronger than he'd ever be.

CHAPTER 6

The drive to Oregon was really, really long. I wasn't much of a road tripping person. At least, I wasn't anymore. Drive here, drive there. By the time we took care of Ross, I would have traveled the country in this motorhome more than I ever desired, and I'd be okay if I never did so again. My plans included staying in the swamp for the foreseeable future. Maybe we could fly places and then fly home. No more driving here, there, and everywhere.

Nope. No thank you.

Jarret leaned over, placing his chin on my shoulder. "Are we going to be able to get you back in the motorhome to return home, or will you refuse to leave because you're never driving again?"

I grinned. "Am I being that obvious?"

"Yep." He smiled. "You are."

I groaned. "Sorry."

I really didn't have a case to complain. I'd showered and eaten. I could even sleep if I wanted to. But I didn't want to.

And the things I wanted to do, I wasn't going to do with my brother hanging out in the front seat and Miranda chatting away like she and Rainer hadn't been ready to kill each other earlier. Of course, he might slaughter her just for never shutting up. We weren't really that much of an extroverted group. Sure, we talked, but we didn't work out our emotions by hashing them out verbally so much as we did on the inside.

That was an interesting observation I hadn't considered before. When my wolf was mate shopping, did she know that the four of them weren't going to be chatty? I didn't think Anton would have been much different if he could speak aloud. We were all pretty much lost in our heads. I preferred it that way.

"We have to stop for gas at the next rest stop," Isaac called out. "And I'm up for snacks."

Isaac was always up for snacks. That hadn't changed since childhood. And his wolf metabolism meant he could eat as much as he wanted. Even when he wasn't shifting. I smiled. "I could eat. I mean, it might be nice to just get out of the vehicle."

"Our girl is getting stir crazy." Preston kissed my cheek as he walked by. "I don't blame her."

Rainer stretched out his legs. "Okay. We'll all get out but be mindful. Nothing with this Loup has made sense. If he's somehow tracking us, he could turn the whole truck stop into some kind of attack zone. I'm really not in the mood." He got up. "Or maybe I am. Come on, Loup, bring it on."

Isaac pulled the motorhome off the highway, stopping pretty quickly after he did. Looked like we had been close when Rainer had made the declaration.

I smiled, even though I should be scowling at him for suggesting such a thing. Before we could go outside, I had to make sure he was clean of the Loup's control. He leaned into my hand, and I closed my eyes, willing my powers to show up if there was anything amiss. Nothing happened, so I grinned as I lifted my lids. "You're golden."

"Only because you're touching me." He dipped me down like I was a heroine from some old romantic movie and passionately kissed me. I giggled against his mouth before I kissed him back. When he finally let me up, I had to stand still for a long second before I fell over because I was slightly dizzy.

That was when my hands started to burn. I gasped, the pain feeling like an assault against the sweet moment Rainer had just given me.

He furrowed his brow. "Is it me? I don't feel him."

I shook my head. "It's no one here."

Miranda pointed at the door. "Let her out."

Yes, that was what had to happen, sooner rather than later. Someone out there needed my help. Isaac pressed the button that opened the door and lowered the stairs. I waited until it was safe and exited to the outside. A dust of rain hit my head, and I shivered. The change in temperature from the inside to the out was significant. Where were we? I hadn't thought to ask, and I didn't even really care. If we weren't there yet, I wasn't concerned.

We were hardly alone. As we were caravanning, our decision to stop had made them all pull off the road, too. Our family members who we had found quickly circled us, asking questions. I couldn't hear any of them. My hands burned, and what was more, I knew exactly where I had to go.

Still, I had to think about doing this safely. "It's not here." I met Anton's gaze. "It's across the highway."

As though in unison, everyone turned in the direction I was looking.

"You have to cross traffic." Jarret sighed. "Should we get back in and move the motorhome?"

"We need to give that thing a name. Like we all start calling it Penelope. Can the motorhome be Penelope?" Preston asked and then quickly spoke again. "Okay, she needs to cross the highway and there is no way for us all to get over there and park. So we help her here. We're all shifting."

Miranda nodded. "Right."

Now she was taking directions from Preston? The power struggles in this wolf existence were real. Was this constant, or just because we were essentially starting over after denying ourselves for so long? I didn't suppose it mattered right now. What mattered was that I had to get to that Loup who was across the highway.

I bounced on my feet. "Should I shift?"

"No," Rainer answered. "You and Anton stay two-legged. He's going to watch your back. I want you to be able to speak to this Loup. I think we need to make a policy to start doing that. We've got the one back at the house waiting for your return, too. They might know things. They have stories. We need to hear them."

Jarret sucked in a breath and spoke low in my ear. "I wish he knew how much he is starting to sound like Cristian. He was so born for this."

I was sure he was. We were all born for this. I kissed his cheek. "Don't get hit by a car."

"I can't believe we're going to run across the highway." Jarret rolled his eyes. "But our lives are never boring. See you over there."

I looked at Rainer. His wolf was in his eyes, he was about to shift. "Why are you running across as wolves?"

"Because if anyone sees anything, they'll just remember

there was a group of wolves rushing across the highway. Nothing to do with any Loups or you. And if we get hit, it won't hurt us much. If it does, you can fix us."

That was all true. "Well, don't get hit anyway. I'm tired of all of you being injured."

"We're tired of you being attacked." He winked at me. "Someday, it'll be better. I know it."

He was lying, and I was letting him. Sure, we'd both pretend we were optimists. It was something that Rainer and I did together. We both knew the opposite was the truth.

They shifted and ran. I rolled my eyes. Talk about total disregard for their safety or that of the oncoming traffic on both sides of the highway. This was a four-lane catastrophe waiting to happen. I couldn't heal the humans, so no one had better be injured or hurt in what could very well count as us participating in vehicular manslaughter.

Of course, it was all my fault.

I sighed. Cars screeched to a stop, pulling off to the shoulders, and I winced in abject horror as they somehow managed not to hit each other. I covered my mouth in awe. The universe had just smiled at us. No one was hurt, no cars had crashed, and it really did look like random wolves were all over the road.

I ran. If anyone noticed, I hoped it wouldn't be for very long. My hands burned. The Loup needed me, and thanks to these amazing people, I could help them. Anton was right behind me. We probably looked like a lunatic couple running with the wolves, or maybe they would think we had something to do with rounding them up. It didn't matter. I was going to disappear into the woods on the other side of the highway, and no one would ever know what happened to me.

It didn't take long with traffic stopped, and I was soon where I needed to be.

Anton followed close but didn't interfere with me. I was grateful for his company. And there was the Loup. He waited like he'd known I would come, and maybe he did. They reached out to me along our psychic link and called for help. I could do no less than help them.

But I was at risk of their madness harming me physically every time I did. I had to be cautious and smart about this, or I was going to have to heal from injury. I was tough and strong, but I'd been through a lot lately. Even at my young age, I wasn't sure how much more I could take.

"What are you doing out here?"

It tilted its head, looking mangled and sick. It broke my heart. I used to be scared of Loups, but these days, they were the lesser of all the concerns I had. This was something I knew how to do.

"Did you know I would come? You did, didn't you? Even I don't know where I am, but you did somehow." I walked toward him. "And I'm going to make you feel better. If you come at me violently, this man behind me, who happens to be one of my mates, is going to hurt you. So control yourself."

I hoped he would listen. Placing my hands on him was an act of faith, but then again, so was my entire existence these days. I had to believe that we'd be okay. It was all about my faith in the idea that we had a real place in the world that we belonged here. That breeding ourselves out wouldn't and couldn't work for us

That we were meant to be here, and I'd come when I did into these abilities to save us. I didn't feel like a savior, and I had no god complex. But I had to believe that I was meant for this, or why was it me? Something about me was right for this job.

I sent my energy to him. His madness swirled around me but didn't infect my soul. He wasn't a hard fix. Not when I'd had to bring back so many from Ross' hell. This was just a run of the mill Loup. Probably some poor soul who was lost because there weren't any Omegas around. We helped keep order in the pack, because when we weren't there, things and people went askew. So all I had to do was see to it that Ross was killed, and then there would be more Omegas born, and in about eighteen years, I could take a break.

Shuddering at the length of time it was going to take, I almost dropped my hands. It was amazing that I could think at all during this time. When I'd first started doing this, it had been really difficult, like I was going to pass out, as though I couldn't endure it. Well, it was nice to know I was getting stronger.

He righted inside, giving me the madness, letting it go. Wasn't that what we all really needed to do when it came down to it? We needed to release what kept us from being our best selves?

The Loup jerked as he let go of his burdens and gave them to me. I stepped back. Anton placed his hand on my back, and I smiled at him. Now would be when I would have fainted in the past or needed to go lie down. I felt no such inclination now.

He lifted an eyebrow in question, and I shook my head. "If you want to carry me you can, just because that is sort of fun and definitely romantic, but not because I'm about to fall on my head."

Anton kissed my shoulder, right on his spot. He loved me, and somehow, he got me when I wasn't sure that I really understood myself. But if someone as inherently good as

Anton thought I was worthwhile, then that went a long way to convincing me that I might actually be able to do this.

The Loup shifted, coming back into his human body. He was an old man, gray-haired, wrinkled. When he opened his eyes, he seemed to view me with clarity. Usually, I didn't see them like this. I was too busy having to be carted off to recover that I never saw the part.

He sat up slowly and I smiled at him. "My name is MacKenzie. This is Anton, one of my mates. How are you feeling?"

The man rubbed his eyes. "I've been looking for you."

That much I knew. "You found me. Well, I found you. But here we are." We needed to get him some clothes and some money so he could move on. I doubted he had anything anywhere if he'd been living like this.

I looked at Anton. "We should have brought clothes and money."

"No." The man got to his feet. "She told me to find you. To tell you in this moment that you have to defeat him by being who you were always meant to be. But not just you. Everyone. Do you understand?"

I really didn't. Squatting down, I met his gaze. He looked down. That was wrong. This wasn't a submissive wolf. He'd just been beaten down. Plus, no one dropped their gaze to the Omega. That was why we were able to help. "Who told you this?"

Maybe he wasn't done needing help, but my hands weren't on fire, so it was probably not something I had to do. He might need some human help.

"My mate. The Omega. She said you would know. I did everything I could to help. I broke him once. That's how you're here. Just one day, when I broke."

I rubbed the back of my neck. I would know?

That was when I saw her, like a vision passing in front of my eyes. I rose and stared. She wasn't really here, but she was an echo. The Omega who visited me in the unconscious. She'd been trying to help from the great beyond. Or wherever it was that happened when this was over. I didn't really know the general thinking about this, and I wasn't sure anyone could say they did. At the end of the day, I was back to the faith issue.

But it didn't matter, because there she was.

I looked at Anton. "Can you see her?"

Or was I asleep and I just didn't know it? Was that possible?

He nodded and took my hand, squeezing it.

"You're ready." She walked toward me. Well, it was more like floating. Her legs were moving like she walked, but she wasn't touching the ground. I was so glad Anton saw this, too. No one would believe me otherwise. Werewolves, yes. Spirit-like things, no.

She stopped near the man I'd just healed and took his hand. I caught my breath. Okay. I was finally catching on. She was an Omega, and he had been her mate. Or still was. I liked the idea that mating was eternal. I wanted to be with mine forever.

"You sent him to me."

"We knew things were ending." The Omega speaking to me turned in my direction. "He volunteered because he's always been so brave. We knew he'd become a Loup without me. He'd have to live like that, but he fought. Messed with the link between all of them and waited for you. You had to be strong, you had to be ready to feel him. When you found him, it would be time for you."

I sucked in a breath. The honking behind me had

stopped. We might be out of time very soon, but I would not rush this. "Time for what?"

"Do you understand what collective knowledge is?" She took another step in my direction, and I took another toward her.

I swallowed. "It's when something is passed on to a group, how they learn it together."

"Sure. Exactly that. When we teach our pups how to fight as a wolf. You never had the benefit of that. But presumably, if you can do this, you will then teach others. It's the collective learning that we pass on and on. The trouble is, there are all kinds of things you'll never be taught as an Omega that might help you. Forget the might, that *would* help you."

I smiled. "Too bad for me, I guess."

Anton squeezed my shoulder, and I turned my smile toward him. He'd be there for me whether I succeeded or failed at this. His love for me didn't have qualifications, and there was such beauty in that it took my breath away. I might not get this done, and that was okay with him. I let myself look at the Omega spirit again. Her mate loved her like Anton did me. He'd ridden through hell because she'd needed him to. I rubbed my arms, cold washing over me. I'd never ask it of mine. They came first, and if that made me a bad Omega, then so be it.

"I'm here in this moment to give you what you need." She was finally right in front of me.

In other circumstances, I'd roll my eyes at that. It sounded like a pickup line, or like something that someone who wanted to sell me something might say. But given things, I actually believed her. Of course, I had no idea what she intended or how that could possibly be.

"You're ready for this."

She touched the side of my face, and I gasped. It burned like my hands did when I was fixing others. Anton tried to yank me back, but it was too late. It was as though the Omega in front of me was glued to the side of my face.

Other than the burn, it didn't hurt. There was no pain, just the feeling like the world had tilted left and wasn't going to tilt back again. Dizziness wafted through me, and my stomach clenched. I might very well puke. But then the sensation passed.

Instead I saw them... Generations of women. They were right there in front of me. One after another. Werewolves, every one of them. Strong. I blinked, and one would change into another one. Time was fluid because somewhere in their eyes, they all held the same spark of knowledge and talent. Did I have that?

The one in front of me shook her head. "You do. But we're going to make sure you have it even more."

I didn't understand. How was my seeing all of them like this supposed to do that for me? I'd no sooner thought the question than the knowledge started to hit my mind. I wasn't just seeing these women, I was being given their memories. They flowed into me. One after another. I could hardly keep up. They'd done a lot of things. More than I could imagine. Healed countless werewolves through times that would bring people to their knees. Wars. Famine. Plagues. Death. Loss. The Omega saw her pack through whatever they needed. The burdens were big, sometimes too much that way, but she stayed there, and she fought until there wasn't anything left in her to give. That was her role, her curse, her blessing. That was who she was.

The Omega was the one for her pack.

My knees threatened to give out, but Anton grabbed me, keeping me upright. And then he wasn't alone. Rainer was there. Preston. Jarret. They'd come looking for us. I couldn't see them right then, but I could feel them. Strong. I wasn't burdened with this alone. The Omega never was. I had strong mates who shouldered anything I asked, and even those things I didn't know I should ask for help with.

If I had chosen this, so had they.

Nothing was too much for them. Not even asking them to become a Loup and hold things until a new Omega could find her way through the blockage a powerful Alpha Loup created. The man I'd saved had done that for his mate.

She stood in front of me now, and I could see her differently. She wasn't just an old woman who visited me in dreams. She'd been strong and should have looked younger than she did when she died. This was what Ross had done to her.

"You tried." I whispered the words. "You battled him."

"I lost." She nodded. "He was so much stronger than me."

Yes. I could see that. He'd drained her—all of them who fell during that time—and taken them from the packs. "How can I be strong if you weren't?"

She held on to my cheek, brushing her thumb over it. "Communal knowledge. I never had it. But then we realized when we were all too weak that there would be a chance if we learned from each other. All of us had been taught from someone who was taught from someone. We carried their wisdom with us, even if we didn't realize it. We talked and talked. I held on to it, all the way to death and sent Winston away, knowing I would be able to reach him, even if I had passed. When you reached him, I would reach you. We had to believe that this was possible. That you were possible, MacKenzie Harper." She smiled. "And you are. Take what we gifted you, and do what must be done."

She gently pulled back her hand. Everything spun and then righted again. I grabbed on to my head just as Preston knelt down in front of me. "Are you okay? What were they all doing to you?"

He'd been able to see all of them. I lifted my head to look past him. The Loup was gone. Where had Winston—that was his name—disappeared to? I hoped it was somehow with his mate. The Omega who orchestrated this from the grave.

Goosebumps broke out on my arms. "I know that you guys will love me if I fail at this." I had to answer Preston, but I needed to say this first. "But I won't be able to live with myself. They came to me from the grave. Or their know-how did. And if I fuck this up, if I don't somehow make this work after all of that, then I am the lowest form of Omega there ever was."

Preston took my hand in his and kissed my knuckles. "I think you answered me."

Rainer finally spoke, only crickets and the sounds of moving traffic on the highway greeted my ears as he did. "I have to challenge him. It will be an Alpha challenge that takes him down. I know it."

I lifted my gaze to meet his. "I don't know, Rainer. He's not an Alpha like we understand the meaning to be. He's different. He can take control of people's minds. How do you think you can possibly beat him like that?"

He shook his head. "We'll know when we know. Isaac managed to park the RV next to the highway. A bit down the road from here. Let's get you settled. And then let's get this son of a bitch."

I loved my pack. We'd chosen each other well.

CHAPTER 7

Anton was driving the RV. My brother, Miranda, and her mate weren't with us. It was the first time we'd all been alone in as long as I could remember. We were headed for hell, but for the first time in forever, I actually found breathing to be easy.

Rainer slipped into the front seat next to him and winked at me on his way up there. Something was up. Rainer really wasn't a winking kind of a guy. I sat on the couch and stared up at Jarret, who stood right in front of me. Apparently, we had thrown the rules of how-to-keep-safe-when-driving out the window. We were all just doing what we wanted now.

"You asked Preston and me a question when we were out on the dock."

Wasn't that a million years ago? "What did I ask?"

"You asked us," he knelt down in front of me, "if we wanted to have sex with you at the same time."

I swallowed. Oh yes, this was all coming back to me now. What a different time that had been, what different things I had been worried about, even though I'd already been in trouble. I just hadn't known how much quite yet.

"Yep," I smiled. "I remember."

"So do we." He leaned over and kissed my cheek. "The answer then and now is that we want to make love to you any way you want to be made love to. Just the fact that we get to touch is amazing to us. But we thought...maybe we could make the rest of the trip more enjoyable for you."

I rose from my seat.

"Really?" I lifted an eyebrow. Jarret stood, towering over me, and I ran my hands over his chest, touching the fabric of his shirt and slightly yanking on it. "Here?"

He pointed behind him. "In the bedroom where Preston is waiting."

I'd assumed he was sleeping, since he'd spent so much time helping my brother drive. I smiled. "Well, I'm game if you're game."

He strung our fingers together and tugged me toward the small bedroom. A lot of things had happened in this tiny motorhome. "I need to remember to thank Gus for this sometime. He did buy it for us, even if he doesn't know that yet, because I doubt he's checking credit card bills."

Rainer laughed, a loud sound. "We'd better warn him. He won't think to look. Hardly ever spends any money. It might come as a shock. He should be warned."

I shook my head. The strong werewolf brought down by a heart attack caused by the spending I did on his credit card.

Anton turned around just long enough to give me a grin. He would pay it off. I knew that in the way that I could just understand what he was saying without him having to say it.

"Thanks." I nodded back at him. "I'll figure out a way to pay you back."

He shook his head and shot me a look over his shoulder that spoke volumes. Anton didn't like that at all. I sighed. "Or I'll just say thank you. And I love you. And thank you, again."

His smile lit up the vehicle. He liked that.

"Hey, lover boy." Rainer groaned. "Eyes on the road or I'm driving."

I grinned at them. I loved these guys, and what was more, I loved being part of their family. That was the thing about mating and becoming pack. It went beyond our having a sexual relationship. We became each other's everything. It was a connection I needed with every breath I took.

Waiting for me in the small bedroom was Jarret, who leaned against the wall, and Preston, who lay shirtless and seemingly relaxed on the bed.

I'd been feeling brave, but the second I saw them, I realized what I'd done. I had no idea how to have a ménage a trois. It had been hypothetical and something I'd speculated about, but never actually imagined doing.

Now, here we were.

"Guys, I'm really a chicken. Bawk. Bawk. Bawk. I just got nervous and..."

Preston put out his hand. "You don't have a cowardly bone in your body. Now, if you don't want to, that is different, but maybe you could see how you like it once we get started. Jarret and I have never done this together before either. We haven't liked other women, and we love you. Just you. So this is a first for us, too."

"But," Jarret stepped toward me, "it's really going to just be us loving you."

I couldn't say no to that. Not in any existence would I dream of turning that down, nerves or no nerves. In fact, I wasn't sure what I had to be nervous about. I loved these men. I'd been with both of them before. I knew how much they wanted me, and even more, I could feel their love pressed against my heart, courtesy of their bites. When those had been taken from me, I'd been empty inside.

But now? Full to the brim.

I pulled my shirt over my head and discarded it. "It's good to face the things that scare us."

"We shouldn't scare you." Jarret took my hand. "We worship you."

And that, in and of itself, was its own kind of frightening. But I'd worry about that later. Jarret kissed me, the gentlest of caresses before he stroked his finger over my nipple, sending jolts of pleasure through my body with just that small amount of touch. Preston got up on his knees, taking my other hand and dragging me toward him to the bed. I tugged Jarret with me, and we all landed on the bed.

I giggled. This was sort of silly, and that made what was left of the discomfort flee. I could do this because it was going to be fun.

"I don't love being the center of attention. I've had a ton of that lately. I'll never get used to it."

Preston pulled me until my back was against his chest, and Jarret stayed face to face with me.

"I feel like I'm in the middle of a sandwich of Lejeune men."

Jarret nuzzled against my shoulder. "As you know, love, when we mated you, we became Harpers."

Yes, I did tend to forget that. In my mind, they would probably always be the Lejeune brothers. My Lejeunes.

Preston pulled down my pants and discarded them next to the bed. I wasn't wearing underwear. With all the constant changing we had to do with the shifts, it just got in the way. Both of my guys were still mostly dressed.

"Am I doing this alone?"

Jarret laughed. "Trust us, we'll get there. For now, just relax."

Whatever I would have said, I lost somewhere in my thoughts because Jarret kissed me as Preston placed a hand on my stomach. Oh yes...I could get used to this sort of thing. They were both touching me at the same time. Sure, that had been the point right off the bat, but the reality of it stole my coherence. Jarret pushed his tongue between my teeth, and I let him. As pleasure flooded me, I moaned against his mouth.

Behind me, Preston gripped me tighter. "Make that noise again. Make it again and again."

He ran his hand up my side, stroking the side of my breast. I sighed, my body relaxing, while at the same time, gearing up for what was going to come next. Preston backed up, letting go of me. "Jarret's going to make you come, and then I am. If you spend all your energy with him, I'm just going to have to get you all excited again."

I swallowed. "Sounds like a plan."

Jarret kissed me, his mouth demanding. He was usually a gentle lover, but this time was different. He consumed my mouth, stole my breath, and I was glad to let him. I'd been so consistently on for so long, this was an incredible moment to truly give myself to him.

He would take care of me for the next little bit, and when he was done, then Preston would. Fuck. I was a lucky woman.

Jarret bent over and sucked on my breast. I sighed before I yelped. Jarret wasn't fooling around. He sucked hard. And I fucking loved it. I bucked beneath him, and he steadied me by grasping on to my arm. His hand wasn't gentle. I could see how this was going to go. I grinned up at him.

"Any way you want it." My wolf rushed to my eyes, and his followed a second later. For a moment, we stared at each other just like that. There wasn't any part of me that didn't adore him. He smiled, and the wolf faded away, returning us both to our human state.

"You're so beautiful, Kenzie. There is no one who touches you. They don't exist. You are everything."

I sucked in my breath. That would sound cheesy if it were coming from anyone but Jarret. He always meant every word he said. I stroked my hand down the side of his cheek, feeling the bite of the shadow of whiskers there. He needed to shave. Or maybe he didn't. I loved him like this.

"I love you."

He smiled at me like I'd just given him the best gift in the world. "Thank you for that. I love you like you made the universe. You know that, right?"

Preston sighed. "I can't talk as well as you do, brother. Stop making me feel less."

I reached my hand toward Preston, and he squeezed it there for a second. I knew his love for me, too. I didn't need his words to feel that from him. Everyone was different. With Jarret, we had to speak.

Preston let go of my hand, and I turned my attention all the way back to Jarret. He smiled down at me. "Take my shirt off."

I nodded. Yes, I'd do that. If he wanted to get a little Alpha right now, I was happy to go down that road. More than happy, ecstatic. I tugged on his shirt until it came off, and I threw it aside. Jarret was strong, lean, and gorgeous. I ran my hand over the mark I'd given him. It was a visible sign of the connection we had on the inside, but it was more than that, too. There was wolf magic to that bite. Once we had it, we needed it to survive.

"I wear your mark with pride."

With that, he kissed me again before he dropped his head to kiss my breast. I shivered, waiting for what was going to happen next. He was going to bite me, and I knew just where that would happen. My nipple. Sure enough, he took a nip right there. I cried out, arching beneath him. Maybe I needed the tinge of discomfort right then. It really looked like I did.

I squirmed, and he let go only long enough to suck on the other nipple. My body heated. Every second that he sucked was sweet torture, and I wanted more.

He ran his hand down my stomach, pausing to cup the little roundness there before he scooted down. I caught my breath. "Jarret, your pants."

"In a second, love."

With gentle hands, he pushed my knees apart until he was clearly where he wanted to be. I smiled. It happened to be that I wanted him right there, too. He kissed both my thighs, and I trembled. I didn't know if I'd ever shaken like this before. He hadn't even really touched me yet. But I was wet, and fuck, I was ready.

He pushed his mouth down on me. I gasped as he moaned. "Kenzie, you taste so good. I crave this."

I couldn't talk because he found my clit with his tongue. I full on shook as he sucked on me. Jarret always knew. I didn't want him poking at me with his tongue. I wanted him to suck, and oh how he got it. He could use his mouth like a pro at this.

The pleasure built up like it had been dammed and now needed to overflow. I grabbed on to the bed, digging my hands into the sheets and holding on to them, like they might somehow keep me from exploding into nothingness.

But it was useless, because I wanted the release. If I shattered because of that, then so be it.

And then it happened. I bucked, nearly kicking him in the head, which made Jarret laugh. I smiled. He pulled up his head to look at me. "I'll take the concussion to know that I pleased you."

Preston's mouth came down on mine. "I love watching you come." He kissed me again. "I want to capture your cries in my mouth."

Jarret shook his head. "Not done yet."

Preston kissed the end of my nose as he spoke to his brother. "Okay." With a groan, Pres rolled over and leaned on his arm. "This is torture. I guess you're teaching me patience."

Jarret shook his head, drawing me to him until I sat on the edge of the bed. What was he doing? I tilted my head but didn't ask my question. Being surprised by Jarret would be fun. I didn't have to worry about what it would be.

"It occurred to me when I was imagining this, that there would be lots of ways to get a really good angle against your most sensitive areas."

I liked where this was going already. "Okay..."

"Lean back, but keep your hips in the air."

I did as he asked while he stripped himself of his pants and underwear. Jarret was hard and huge. I wanted to reach forward and stroke him from tip to his balls, but he was too far for me to reach in the position where he'd left me. His gaze held my own as he breathed fast. If he was even aware that Preston was in the room anymore, I couldn't tell.

Jarret could hyper-focus, and it was my luck that he was doing it right now on me.

He shifted until his cock was positioned right where he wanted it, and then he thrust inside of me. I wasn't imaginative, so I really wouldn't have known that my hanging off the edge of the bed while he pushed inside of me would give me such a rush, but there it was. Every move and jerk of his body brought pleasure to me as it rubbed against my clit.

I grabbed on to his arms. "Jarret."

"Too much?" He tilted his head, and I shook my head fast. I absolutely did not want him to stop.

"Just like that. That rhythm."

His smile was warm. "I'm always yours to command."

It didn't take long to get me worked up, but I also didn't want it to end. I squeezed him tighter every time he entered me, and when he pulled out, it was like a loss. But I wanted more, so much more, and I was happy to beg for it, only he wasn't making me do that.

No, Jarret was giving me just what I needed, because that was always what he did. He understood me, he made me know myself better. With every thrust and burst of pleasure, I had clarity in the ways that he loved me and the ways that I adored him. It was complete and all consuming.

I could hardly breathe from the beauty. It was all mixed up in my love for him, and when I finally came, the release was so sweet, it came with tears. Someone else might have been freaked out by them, but when they burst from my eyes, Jarret leaned over and kissed them off my face, murmuring sweet nothings when he did. When he came inside me, it just cemented the moment, the need, the owning of each other the way that we did.

His smile as he adored me with his eyes was slow. "You are everything."

He pulled out of me slowly and planted one long, wet, beautiful kiss on my lips before he moved off me entirely. I was tugged back into Preston's embrace. He kissed the top of my head as Jarret climbed in next to me on the other side.

"He's right," Preston kissed my temple. "You are everything."

I needed to catch my breath. "Just give me a second."

"There's no rush, Mac." He ran a hand through my hair. "None whatsoever. We're just going to lie here for a second."

It was funny, really. I'd never given that much thought to what a ménage encounter would be like. It hadn't really been on my radar as I'd gone through life. But I guessed I thought it would be a lot of throwing each other around and rushing through things. They were holding me now like we had nowhere to go, and Preston still hadn't really gotten to do anything at all yet.

I lifted my head to kiss him, and he met me lips to lips. His were soft, and he sighed against me when I made the contact. "Everything he said?" Pres whispered. "Count me in on that, too. You know I won't be able to say it as pretty as he did."

Jarret laughed. "You make yourself understood just fine."

Preston shoved him lightly on the shoulder. "Funny."

I smiled into Preston's shoulder before I climbed on top of him. He was still fully clothed, but I straddled him just the same. I was sweaty and messy. He was going to have to change his clothes. I doubted he'd care.

I leaned over to kiss him, brushing my nose over his chin and cheeks before I did, just so I could really breathe him in. "He's right, you know, Preston. You make yourself under-stood perfectly well. And I love what you say."

Not tired or languid anymore, I kissed him hard. Preston needed to be shown just how much I valued him, and I was glad to do that anytime, anywhere. That thought struck me. I would do it any place he wanted. My smile was fast. There was something sort of fantastic about realizing I was that kind of person. I might not have as many boundaries as I'd previously imagined.

A whole new MacKenzie Harper. Or maybe I was being ridiculous and I should just make love to Preston and not overthink this.

"I want your clothes off, Mr. Harper." There, I'd called him Harper and resisted the urge to say Lejeune. His smile was huge and told me he'd noticed.

He ran a hand through his hair. "Sure. Because you got the name right."

I winked at him. "Is that the only reason?"

Running my hands over his chest—I loved his strong muscles—I massaged the mark that made him mine.

"Maybe that isn't the only reason. Maybe there are many." He kissed my neck. "Mac, I'm going to need you to get off my lap if you want me to strip off my pants."

That was a good point. I dramatically sighed and rolled off him onto the bed, which put me right next to Jarret. I stared at him for a long second. He had his eyes closed but he wasn't sleeping, more like he was lying there with contentment.

He opened his eyes and winked at me. "It does take getting naked to have sex."

I laughed just as Preston pulled me back over him. "Now, where were we?"

Okay. We weren't the smoothest crew to ever have sex like this, but I wouldn't trade these laughing moments for anything in the world. There was such joy in being with them in this uncomfortable bed while we made this up as we went along. I knew I'd never forget it, and even if it would never find its way into some how-to book on group sex, I'd take these moments over anything else in the world.

He was hard, and I was more than ready. I sat up higher,

but just so I could fit him inside of me before I pressed down. He cried out, making the best gasp I'd ever heard. That was the thing with Preston. Every time felt like the first time with him. He was always so surprised to be inside of me, and that was really wonderful. Everyone should know this kind of adoration. It should be a requirement for life, to know that the person you were with wouldn't trade you for anything in the universe.

Preston took control of my hips, setting my pace, and I let him. Yes, he was right, the angle and the movements were better. He got to rub me the way I needed, and he got harder and harder with each pass.

Oh the power in knowing I could make him this needy. I threw my head back, grasping my own breasts in my hands and squeezing my nipples. Preston let out a long moan. I guessed he liked that. Or no guessing about it, he fucking did.

We banged against each other. I let go of my breasts to hold on to his shoulders as we dug and dove into each other's bodies. I'd never been closer with him. He pressed his forehead to mine, and it was like we were breathing together. Every in and out we took was joined. I finally couldn't stand it anymore.

"I need..."

Somehow, he knew without me having to finish that thought. Preston placed a finger between us, stroking my clit for a long second. I exploded. Yes, I'd needed that. But then I couldn't breathe. I could just exist in the universe where Preston was taking me hard. My body clenched around him, as I had no control over what my muscles did. I couldn't have thought thoroughly enough to have made anything happen just then.

With one last jerk, he spent himself inside of me. Tears

sprung to my eyes again, and I let them fall. This was a day for crying, for beautiful tears to show how beloved I was to these men that I had made my own.

"Love you," Preston whispered in my ear. "Always will."

I believed him.

Time blurred for me. Eventually, I lay on the bed, snuggled between Jarret and Preston, embraced in their warmth. It was a great feeling to float in giddiness.

Preston started to snore, and it dragged me out of my haze. I smiled. He was always telling me to kick him, but I wasn't going to do that. Ever. Who wanted to be kicked?

Jarret leaned up on his arm. "One time we were on a vacation, which was weird for my family. We didn't go anywhere because my mom was so afraid of someone coming to take Anton, but Gus insisted. So we all went on this camping trip. He and I ended up in a tent. Longest night of my fucking life."

I shook my head. "I like the sound. It tells me he's there."

"See? I love my brother, but you are in love with him. Totally different thing. I'll kick him for you."

I rolled my eyes. "I wouldn't kick you either."

"You're also in love with me." He rubbed his eyes. "I'm hungry. Are you hungry?"

His saying it made me suddenly aware of just that. "Yes. Starved."

"Let's see if we can get Rainer to make grilled cheese."

I loved that idea. And even knowing that it was all going to be really, really hard shortly couldn't diminish my happiness.

CHAPTER 8

G oose Lake in Oregon was beautiful. It wasn't anywhere I'd ever planned to visit. But there I was, standing on the side of the lake, wondering where to go from there. Rainer handed me a sweater, and I smiled at him.

"Thanks." I nudged him. "I have no idea where he is by the way. I'm here, but I don't have a deep-seated internal radar that tells me where he is."

I couldn't feel a tug or anything. He might not even be here for all that I knew. We'd brought a caravan of wolves to Oregon from Louisiana, and I didn't have a clue if I'd just given us all a massive ride in the car for no good reason. Of course, it hadn't been me. It had been my guys, but I grouped myself with them. What they did, I did. It just sort of worked like that.

If I'd been conscious, I'd have gone right along with what they'd decided.

"He's here." Rainer rocked back on his feet. "And it won't take long for him to notice that we are and have a temper tantrum about it. Things will take a sharp left turn soon."

"How do you know?"

"I just do. I can feel the challenge coming." He lifted an eyebrow. "In the end, it will be him and me in an Alpha challenge. Let's hope I can beat an old Alpha who has garnered more power over the years than he was entitled to."

The wolf rushed into my eyes, and his joined me. Rainer might not know it, but his was smiling right now. I grinned back at him. Our wolves had no question about his strength. His wolf was one hundred percent certain he could best any challengers, win any war. There was a strut to him that Rainer in his human form simply didn't have.

Ross the Loup had seen to that with the Accords, when they'd beaten him down emotionally, framed him for something he hadn't done, and sent him to prison. That had kicked the shit out of my Alpha. But his wolf had held on, even in the years of never shifting. He'd waited, and in this moment that would be coming, he knew himself to be strong enough.

Plus he had me, and I had generations' worth of Omega knowledge to see me through what I had to do.

He wasn't telling me how he would kill the Loup, and I wasn't letting him know what I intended to do to help. This was a funny moment. If either of us broke our silence, the other might try to interfere, might get worried. Staying mutually close-mouthed made this an equally thought out choice to not burden each other with what had to be done.

Our wolves understood it, and even though I didn't consciously know what Rainer intended to do, my wolf trusted his. And so therefore, I did as well.

That was the beauty of the dual nature of ourselves. We could relate on many levels, and all of them made sense in a way I couldn't have fathomed.

My wolf pulled back and so did his. I didn't have to tell him that I believed in him. I just had, and not with words.

"MacKenzie..." His smile was soft. "What happened with you and Jarret and Preston on the motorhome..."

I lifted my eyebrows. Where was he going to go with this? "Yes?"

"Not for me, okay? I want to be that person like Jarret and Preston. But I can't be. At least, not yet. When it's you and me being intimate, can we keep it just you and me? I'm so glad you all had fun and wanted that." He cupped my cheek. "I get so little time with you alone, and I don't want to be disappointing, so if it's important to you, then..."

I kissed his chin, and he stopped talking. "You could never be that. And yes, it can just be us. There are no rules about this having to be a constant group...romp." I wasn't sure if that was the right word, but I was using it because it would get my point across. "I don't think they'd want that either. I think that was them fulfilling a request I made earlier. I don't think it was on either of their lists."

Rainer kissed my cheeks. "They'd never have done anything they didn't want to do. You asked the right two. I can't speak for Anton, but I didn't get the impression while we were driving that he was anxious either. So maybe we're selfish with you."

I shook my head. "You two are absolutely not that."

He wrapped his arms around me and held on. I closed my eyes and sighed. This might be one of the greatest hugs I'd ever had. Rainer was great that way. He didn't give affection looking for it to become something else. I'd heard women in the hair salon where I'd swept up talk about that. They never could have a kiss or a hug that didn't turn into sex with their partners. That wasn't what Rainer did. It was as though he understood my need for affection that was just that, affection.

Not that I'd complain if we were to end up having sex either, but this wasn't the time for that. I was glad for his strong arms.

"Whatever happens..." His voice sounded hoarse. "I wouldn't trade a minute of what we've had together." I tugged back to argue with him about thinking dour thoughts, but he continued to speak, his words drawing me into what he saw in a way that stole my breath. "You showed up with Gus, and at first, I couldn't believe he'd done that. Rescued you and brought you to Preston? I mean, he didn't even know that the rest of us would be there when he'd made that decision."

I hardly remembered that time. I'd been so completely out of it. "I don't remember you being that thrilled."

"No, we'd fought all day with Preston. Anton wanted him to come home. He wasn't going to do that. I was feeling completely off balance being there at all, and Jarret was a shell of himself." He sighed. "But then you came, my beautiful mate. And I didn't know it yet, but you were going to make everything better. You have, time and again, taken care of us. Now it's our time to help you."

I shook my head. "Are you under the impression you haven't done that? I mean, I was pretty much comatose for days. And yet, here I am."

He winced. "That was Jarret and Anton. I didn't do anything but encourage them to try. And Preston worked this out, where to go. How to do it. That's all them. Now it's going to be my turn."

I squeezed his hands in my own, loving the slight roughness of the callus on his fingers. "Rainer, you don't need to feel like you..."

That was when I felt them. The Loups. I dropped Rainer's hands and swung around to see what had happened. My hands burned. Loups surrounded us.

"Well, I see what you mean about him throwing a fit."

Rainer sighed. The first time we'd seen Loups, we'd all been asleep in our home, lying on mattresses on the living room floor. They'd forced the first shifts on Jarret and Anton, scaring the crap out of the rest of us. We'd all shifted and battled. Rainer had restrained himself from killing two.

Now, he was sighing. Oh, how things had changed.

I put my hands on my hips, even as they burned, ignoring the feeling. I'd gotten better at letting some of the urge to immediately fix wane, and the knowledge of the dead Omegas helped, too. I just had to breathe through the urge

There were ten of them.

That was more than I'd handled all at once before, but I'd cleared entire rooms of the control Ross had over them, so I supposed this wouldn't be very different.

"Do you suppose that Omegas could be born tomorrow?" I shook my head. "Like we kill Ross today and a hundred of them are born tomorrow? Then I just have to wait eighteen years for some help."

Rainer actually laughed. "I don't think there are one hundred werewolves pregnant right now."

"That's too bad."

But it turned out I was really not alone. Growls sounded everywhere, and I swung around to look. Anton. Jarret. Preston. Isaac. Agustin. My mother, which took me a hot second to digest. All of the Lejeunes. Miranda. Her mates. We weren't just surrounded by Loups. Oh no, they were ready to get into the fray of the whole thing with our makeshift pack.

I put my hands out in front of me in the universal sign for stop before I spoke. "Okay. Thank you. We don't need to hurt them. The thing Ross doesn't understand is that he doesn't control them, not really. I do. No amount of control he has will ever circumvent what they need from me." I tilted my head. "But if you guys could herd them like sheep, I'd be so grateful. Bring me one at a time."

Anton moved forward, but my mother beat him to it. I smirked. She was going to have a hard time taking a step back from me when this was over. She pushed her Loup toward me, grabbing on to his leg until he was right in front of me.

I smiled. It was funny. I knew it was she, and yet I'd seen her as a wolf for just seconds once before. But I knew it the way that wolves knew these things. The brown wolf with white spots was my mother. And she was dragging a Loup by the leg.

Chalking that in the column of things I never expected to see was one of the things I'd do today. I stepped forward, placing my hands on the Loup's arms. His pain hit me, but there was something more. Ross had a strong hold on this Loup. Maybe it was the fact that he was so physically close to this Loup, or maybe he'd pushed his strength more than ever before.

I growled, my wolf coming to my eyes. She wanted to shift. We could do all of this on four feet, but I was going to wait on that for later. A vision struck me. It was of an older Omega. She'd been gray haired and blue eyed. It was like she spoke to me in that moment.

She leaned against a wooden pole, like she stood on an old-fashioned porch. Dressed in a green dress with white gloves, I wondered if she was on her way somewhere where she had to look fancy, or if she'd ripped such a lovely dress off every time she'd had to shift. I might never put on good clothes again.

"The thing about a rope is that it can be pulled on both ends. You just have to make it taut and yank it harder. Sometimes, a Loup is still too connected to the Alpha that failed him to begin with you. Have to yank harder, you have to become the thing that they hold on to until you can set them right again."

I loved the slight lilt in her voice. It made me wonder about her background, where she had to have picked up that way of speaking. As far as I knew, we'd all lived in the swamp area and then gone from there, but she would have had to have been somewhere else entirely to sound like that.

I smiled. There was so much knowledge lost in our history, and no one left to teach it to us. Centuries of werewolf understanding disappeared with the death of our people to the Accords. Thanks to the Loup still causing me a headache now.

I pushed myself back to the present. Rainer tilted his head looking at me. "You okay?"

"Just doing a little post-mortem communication."

He shook his head. "So weird."

"Yep. That's a good way to describe it." But I had something to do, and later, we could focus on how odd everything was. Maybe someday I'd just get to be a werewolf, shifting when I wanted to and living an otherwise normal life. Well...maybe. I was going to spend my life with four very hot men in a relationship that was more solemn than most human marriages. That was a different kind of normal.

In the meantime, I focused on the wolf my mother held for me. I had to disconnect him from his Loup and tug harder. My powers were like a wolf with sharp claws. I struck out with them, severing Ross from this man's mind, and then I pushed my healing magic at him so strongly, it was like a growl surging from my mouth. With a smile, I healed him as he gave himself over to me. I lifted my head to Rainer.

"Got him."

My alpha mate smiled, slowly. "I can feel him. You gave him to me."

For now, that was how it would work. What was mine was, as it was, his. "Take him."

"Will do." He nodded. "Bring her the next one."

I wasn't the least bit tired. I could do this all day.

A roar sounded in my head. Everyone around us jumped, even in their wolf bodies, which told me that I wasn't the only one who could hear it. No. I amended that thought. Rainer didn't jump. He tilted his head in the way that he did when he found things interesting but not concerning.

"Someone is mad."

The growls sounded everywhere. I didn't blame them. It wasn't any fun having Ross in their heads. They'd all suffered through that once. But this was different. It wasn't control. It was projection. He'd yelled psychically loud enough through the link that we'd all heard it.

I imagined that was everywhere. Wolves who had no idea what was going on in the middle of who knew where must have heard that noise. A roaring wolf. I preferred the sounds of growls and howls. Much more natural. But Ross had put away everything that was understandable a long time ago.

Closing my eyes, I let myself see him in my mind's eye.

"MacKenzie?" Rainer asked, wanting my attention. He wouldn't like this, me giving any part of myself over to see that Loup.

I lifted my lids and patted his arm. "I'm okay. Ross is in his house. It's very close. I can practically see him, but he's going to wait because I'm busy right now."

"Next up," Rainer called. "Bring her the next one."

I was an Omega. Ross would have to wait his turn for my attention.

When I'd yanked the last of his Loups away, I stood straight up, stretching my back. Anton shifted back and walked toward us as Preston and Jarret stayed in their wolf forms. Preston rubbed against my leg, and I petted him between his ears like he was a friendly canine and not capable of biting off my hand if he so desired. Of course, he wouldn't do that to me. But someone else? He just might. And I loved that about him.

Jarret growled at Gus. I wasn't following their conversation, but something unpleasant must have just been communicated in their wolf forms.

Anton swung around to stare at them and then shrugged at me. Whatever was going on, Anton wasn't that concerned about it. Maybe Jarret and Gus fought a lot. Perhaps this was some level of normal for them.

"Ready?" I looked between Anton and Rainer.

"We are." Rainer spoke as Anton nodded, taking my hand and placing it over his heart. I felt the strong beat for just a second. If life was moments, and our future never guaranteed, then I was going to appreciate every single second that I got to feel their hearts beat.

"How do you want to handle it?" Rainer looked over the group. "This is your call, up until the point that I have to challenge him."

My call. It always was because I was the only Omega born, so it was always going to be me. "Do you think that I'll resent it when I have other Omegas around? Like I'll be like, hey I'd really like this to be a forever solo gig?"

Anton threw his head back. He clearly found that funny. With a tug, he dragged me to him, and I got his implication perfectly the way I always did with Anton. If I ever found myself craving to do this alone, he would see to it that I was seriously distracted.

In the best possible way.

It was funny, really. I was going to go into a battle with an enemy so powerful, he'd destroyed the lives of countless werewolves, hurt my family and those I loved, while also managing to trap me in my own head under his control. But I was perfectly calm.

Was that a good sign or a bad one?

I supposed only time would tell.

With no choice, I dropped Anton's hand. Despite my rather Zen feeling about this, I couldn't go beat Ross while Anton held my hand in solidarity. I was going to have to do this somewhat alone.

Even though a crowd surrounded me.

I bit down on my lip. I should really say something, only it didn't feel like I was the one who should speak right now. Werewolves surrounded me. I needed to be one, too. So I let the wolf into my eyes.

Most of the time when I did that, I didn't really see things differently than I did in my human form. This was different.

They weren't just random wolves. They were mine. I jolted at the thought. I'd known it, but now, I could feel what pack meant to me. It went beyond Rainer, Preston, Jarret, and Anton. They were my mates. That was a separate category. But pack meant more than just family. It was existence. It was where I was meant to place myself in an ever-shifting world. They were *mine*.

It was different than they were Rainer's. If he cared for their physical selves, I was in charge of their emotional lives. I wouldn't let them become Loups. They'd never be lost to madness, not with me in their pack.

I'd learned from generations of Omegas, and I knew one thing and one thing only—I wasn't going to take myself from these souls who had come with me. I wouldn't live in a house where no one knew if I lived or died, showing up only if someone needed me. I was going to fill my days with them.

By my side, I'd have Rainer and his strength, leadership. Preston, and his sense of humor and ability to see through any situation to the core. Jarret and his deep-seated empathy and fast, sharp mind. Anton and the way he seemed to see everything, know things before anyone else.

I was the luckiest Omega ever with them.

But I intended to live a full life surrounded by whatever our pack looked like. We couldn't be taken over by an Alpha Loup if we didn't isolate ourselves into the position where no one spoke so no one realized what was happening.

I wasn't going to be separate from; I was going to be in the mix of all of it. I wouldn't die with no one noticing.

Of course, I could be taken down in just a few minutes and then my grand thoughts would be for nothing.

"We're wolves. We aren't meant to cower. We aren't meant to be locked in cages at the will of one Alpha."

I itched to shift but held myself as I was for a few moments more.

"The first thing we are asked to do when we are adult werewolves is to swear allegiance to our Alpha." I'd never done that, and it seemed like something we should do quickly when this was over. What little I understood about customs, I'd gleaned that much over the years. "And that man took that from us. Sure, he took a lot more than that, but let's start with the fundamental disruption of our choice. None of us picked that man to control us. None of us decided to give him the power over our lives that he has taken without permission." My skin burned. I wanted the shift, and I wanted it now. But I would be more effective against Ross if I didn't give in. Fighting was not my role today. "Today, we take it back. "

They howled, and I smiled. It looked like they were on my side. I wasn't surprised. I could count on them.

"Let's go get him. What I need from you is the ability to get to Ross. He's well protected. These Loups we had here will not be the last, and the ones to come will be violent. Try not to kill them, but do so if you have to." Decisions like these couldn't be easy, and it wasn't for me to say that. I'd always regret the need, and maybe today could end without their deaths. "Rainer and I have to get to Ross. As soon as we have Ross, those Loups will stop fighting. Our missing family members will be freed. This nightmare will be over."

More howls met my announcement. I smiled. "So follow me."

It turned out I knew exactly where he was. I looked over my shoulder. Not only could I feel his glare as though he were there with me, but I'd seen his dock in my head endlessly. When he'd created his fake environment, he'd put me right on his very real dock, albeit the one I'd been on had been in his mind. But there it was. Just close enough, he could see us if he wanted to.

And I was sure he wanted to. I stepped away from the group toward the edge of the lake. It was practically dried up. Was that normal for the area? Maybe it was, maybe it wasn't. It had been nice and full in his mind's creation of this spot. Now, if he tried to throw me into it, I wasn't going to get particularly wet. It would be more like slipping into a puddle. It might have been uncomfortable, but I wasn't going to drown.

What did that tell me? I smiled. He was a lot tougher when he got to make the rules in his land of make believe than when he was out here with the rest of us.

I pointed at the house. "He's there. And if you see any humans, remember he controls them, too. He's a bully, and he shoves his mind against those he can beat up and makes their life hell. But he's just an Alpha who has gotten out of whack. We pick our Alphas. We haven't picked him."

And if I truly did decide to be an Omega, if I really did in some unconscious state sign up for this life, then I was going to make sure I was the best damned Omega for this strange, unpredictable time. So help me, I'd tear apart the world before I let this fucker hurt one more werewolf on my watch. I was the Omega for this time, I'd be whatever it took to protect us.

They were all mine. In the best possible way.

CHAPTER 9

I'd predicted he'd send wolves after us, and I was right. Much as I wanted to shift, I stood in my human form with Rainer in his and watched as our wolves fought the Loups Ross controlled. I itched to fight so much that I had to clench my jaw hard to keep from doing it, and I was rapidly giving myself a headache.

It was a quiet walk, and I found myself scanning for humans, just as the Loups seemed to appear around us. My hands were already burning, but I suspected that the more powerful I became, the less that mattered. I was always ready to handle a Loup. I didn't need my hands to alert me to their presence.

Jarret growled and lunged forward, taking down the first Loup in his way. He grabbed on to the scruff of his neck, and I winced, thinking how disgusting that must taste. Some things were better when I was in my full-on wolf form. I wouldn't consider that sort of thing if I could shift.

Rainer lifted an eyebrow at me as more and more sick werewolves charged out of the house. It was amazing that his neighbors hadn't caught Ross with that many Loups hanging around. Or maybe they were all under his control.

"Ready?"

I nodded but a thought had dawned on me, and I needed to deal with that, too. "Anton," I called out to him, and he swung around, letting the Loup he'd been dealing with go. Preston immediately grabbed the sick wolf and dragged him toward the water. Was he going to drown him? I flinched. I couldn't deal with that. I had to trust them to know what they were doing.

Anton strode over to me quickly, and I bent over to stroke the fur under his chin. "They'll have guns. He didn't have them shoot at us very much, but the humans who will be next will have guns. Take proper precautions. I won't have anyone hurt, and I can't fix anyone until after I'm done with Ross."

He nodded once and then head butted me. I laughed. This was such a serious time. Nothing should have been funny, except that it was.

They'd all follow Anton's lead. He didn't have to talk when he was a wolf, they could all understand him perfectly, like I could all the time. There was something beautiful about our lives. If the humans could understand without terror, they'd envy us our connection. In so many ways, they lived lonelier lives.

"Ready?" Rainer asked again.

"I am."

I was sure of it.

I walked ahead of Rainer, swerving out of the way of wolves fighting to subdue Loups. I darted left, getting swiped at by a Loup twice my size. I rubbed at the wound for a second as it stung, seeing my own blood on my fingertips. It all came down to blood, always. To DNA. The ways that we were the same, the ways that we were different. Somehow, it brought on our psychic connection.

Ross understood that. He used it against us, took Anton as a baby. Maybe others, too. I'd know soon. He wouldn't exploit our strengths and make them weaknesses again. If nothing else, he'd exposed us to humans. The scientists who'd directed us. He'd taken the wolves he'd controlled and sent them on missions to increase his financial worth.

That was so repulsive to me that it created a bad taste in my mouth—the same as what Jarret must be tasting having bit into the Loup.

He would pay. As wolves, we didn't have judges or juries. We were all each other's peers. And I was the Omega.

I wasn't offering him forgiveness.

I stepped through the door.

Gunshots rang out behind me, and I almost turned around. Rainer put his hand on my shoulder. "Don't. Trust them to handle themselves."

They were wolves who hadn't been wolves again for long, if they ever had been before. Maybe some things were natural. I nodded. I couldn't be everywhere. I had my role. They needed to play theirs.

The house was a mess. Things were strewn everywhere, and the smell of Loup was everywhere. Acrid. It made my nose burn to match my hands.

"The Omega is always a strong woman. But she's never alone."

One of the Omegas in my mind whispered in my ear. I didn't know which one. The floor creaked as I stepped over things to get out of the way of the overturned furniture, frayed rugs, and broken glass. It could have been the Loups who did this, but I had a feeling it was just one all on his own.

On the outside, Ross looked like a put together man, but the inside had madness. Centralized, focused madness. His external environment matched his inner turmoil. I felt all sorts of smart for thinking that. Of course, it could also be that he'd had some kind of fit and thrown his shit around. I wasn't a psychiatrist. Just an Omega trying to figure things out.

I made it to the backdoor and paused. "Rainer, this could go one of two ways."

"No." His tone told me he was resolute, and his scent was hard, focused, like he held only determination in that moment. It was a spicy scent, like cinnamon. "There's only one way that it goes."

I put my hand on the backdoor's knob. I couldn't see outside. Ross had closed the blinds. Yet, I knew exactly what I'd be walking into. I didn't need my eyes to see. I had hundreds of Omegas to clear my view.

"Rainer, what do I smell like to you?"

He tilted his head. "Like heaven. The same way you always do."

I should roll my eyes. I'd asked a question, wanting to know if I gave off the cinnamon focus, too, and he'd handed me poor cheese, but since I loved it and believed he thought that, I grinned at him instead.

I opened the door and stepped outside. Ross stood at the end of the dock. The lake looked different, and that wasn't the only other change. Five Loups flanked him. I had Rainer behind me. I guessed we'd both decided not to come alone.

Tug. I heard several Omegas speak, and I nodded, appreciating the help. I would have done it anyway. Yanking and pulling at connections was something I knew how to do now, but I'd never say no to someone confirming my play.

Even if those people were dead Omegas who existed in my self-conscious.

Five at once was a lot to do in terms of tugging, so I raised my hand to give myself a visual. Was it possible to just shift one body part? I stared at my hand and fed my wolf energy. I wanted my claws. Even if I were metaphorically striking and not actually using the claws, I wanted the strength my wolf could give my hand without actually shifting the rest of my body.

My hand obeyed my command and shifted into a paw. It was slightly bizarre to see my hand like that. I might have to experiment with the ability at another time. I had human eyes seeing part of my wolf body. The dichotomy of all of this was a little bit bizarre. But such was life.

I didn't have time for these kinds of musings. Ross' Loups ran at me. This time, I could physically see their tether to him like they were ropes. That was interesting. Was that because of the Omegas, or because I'd partially shifted? I had no idea, not really. With my shifted hand, I cut through the air, severing those ropes that tied them to him.

Power surged through me. Yes, I was made to do this. It was my birthright. The Loups staggered backwards, one of them falling into the lake. I wanted to heal them. That was my job, but it wasn't time yet.

I wouldn't be an Omega left to be slaughtered because I was constantly selfless and all-giving. That wasn't real. No one could be that all the time. If they claimed they could, they were lying.

Rainer stayed silent. He couldn't like this. In the past, he'd been very clear that he didn't want me fighting. But we had no choice here, and there wasn't anyone to do this but me. I was bleeding. I didn't care. I just kept walking toward him. Step by step. One after another. Sometimes that was all we had in life, the next right step.

"How nice to see you. In the flesh." I looked Ross up and down. He'd portrayed himself in the visions accurately. This was exactly what he'd looked like before. In his day, before the madness, he'd probably been an impressive Alpha.

He growled, his eyes turning wolf. They were red-rimmed, Loup eyes. If I'd any question—and I hadn't—there would have been an answer then. He was a mad Loup, and he had to be handled.

I'd never helped an Alpha Loup, and I had to assume that this was going to be a lot more complicated. I had generations of knowledge to call from, but I didn't know if any of them had ever done this. Surely, someone had. Maybe it would come to me when I needed it. Maybe I was all on my own.

Only, I knew better than that. I had four tethers to my heart that Ross had fucked with when he'd taken them away from me. It was my fault I'd temporarily lost my marks, but it was his fault that happened to begin with.

He'd fucked with our lives.

"Things have been hard for you." I was practically right in front of him then. So close, I could have stroked my hand down his cheek if I wanted to. But I didn't. The last thing I wanted to do was to touch that Loup. It wasn't his fault he got sick and lost his way. It was his fault he'd taken it out on the rest of us.

We weren't responsible for the pain in his life, and he could have reached out for help instead of destroying those who helped him. The Omegas were all dead except for me.

For them, I did what I had to do.

I wrapped my arms around him. He struggled, but I held on. Rainer was with me. If need be, he would subdue him without being asked to so I could finish what had to be done. And if something went wrong, I had no doubt that Preston, Anton, and Jarret would somehow know through our connection and come.

I closed my eyes and pushed my energy into him. It was positively mind boggling, but in order for Rainer to beat him in an Alpha challenge, I had to make him a true Alpha again. I had to heal him to finally be rid of him.

Hold on and don't let go. One of the Omegas spoke in my head. Something she had done in her lifetime when she'd had to grab on to a Loup she'd taken care of. Yes, she and I shared the uncomfortable experience.

But this was mine alone. My mind traveled as I pressed energy into him. It had never happened before. He was an Alpha and hundreds of years old. Things were bound to be different. Our minds melded together until I could see what he saw.

He stood in the forest. I could see him not through his own eyes, but as though I was there with him. How was that possible?

Memory is energy... It's stored. The Earth remembers.

One of the other Omegas apparently understood this. I sighed. It was beyond my ability to grasp. I just had to ride through and hope that I came out the other side. I'd study the hows and whys later. I'd go to school until any of it made sense. It didn't matter now. I could see him.

Maybe he was fifteen. Maybe he was younger. It was hard to tell. Wolves grew fast and strong earlier. We were made for strength, and the males were brawny a lot earlier than their human counterparts. But I just had the feeling he was fifteen. Like that was a memory carried somewhere that I'd picked up on.

He was only alone for a second. Soon, he was

surrounded by a lot of other teenagers and younger wolves. His eyes stayed detached, like he wasn't really looking at them. Then, his gaze changed, and his features scrunched up for a second before he seemed to still himself and smile at the others.

I tried to judge what I was looking at. It was as though they were drawn to him, but he didn't know what to do with them. As though their presence caused him pain instead of joy. They wanted him, probably could already sense the Alpha in him, but didn't know it yet. The way Preston described Rainer when he was young, it was as though the charisma was always there. He was meant to lead them. They could feel it in their cells.

But he didn't feel it.

The scene changed, and I cringed against the pain. I didn't know how he did the mind control he managed. This fucking hurt. I squeezed his arms tighter. No matter the discomfort, I wasn't going to let him go.

He was older now, sitting in a room. People were talking to him. I made out bits and pieces of their conversations. Little things they said. Words. They were asking for advice and help. His eyes were dead.

I couldn't scent him. I didn't have that power in this weird memory zone, but I'd lived as a human lived for a long time. I could tell from his gaze a lot about him. He was lost and not present in the moment. The look changed. He wasn't removed anymore. No, he was angry. If I'd really been there, I'd have backed off. Why didn't the people around him know what was happening? They couldn't tell from his gaze? And even if that was the case, why didn't they know from his scent? It had to reek in there of hatred. I'd only scented it once on Preston when he'd been under the control of this monster.

Why didn't they know?

They couldn't smell it. Neither could I.

I couldn't see the face to go with the voice of the Omega who spoke to me. But Ross must have both heard and recognized it. He shook like he recognized it. Wow. That was a big change.

On the dock, while he waited for me to do my job, Rainer called out my name. "MacKenzie?"

"Kenzie?" Jarret must have been with him.

They were comfort, but not what I needed right then. I had to hold on.

The scene changed, but Ross was the same age as he'd been in the last memory. A woman stood in front of him, her hands on her hips. "Mate? I'm not your mate. I doubt you have one. There is something wrong with you, and since you won't let me fix you, I can't tell what it is. Ross, you're not fit to be anyone's mate."

Inside, I gasped. Okay. So some things were starting to make sense. He had wanted to mate an Omega, and she had rejected him. Like *that*?

Oh, hell.

Yes, it wasn't my finest moment, but I couldn't have known.

Her voice in my head. That woman hadn't just rejected him, she'd humiliated him. Okay. To be fair, no one could have foreseen what would happen. Not a single one of us had a crystal ball. We were all making this up as we went along, and she didn't have what I had—the benefit of all those who came before me.

Still, couldn't she have done better than that?

I didn't need to see anymore. I could see the path as it had gone. Quasi lost from an early age, brought to the edge by an Omega who didn't love him, didn't want to mate. He wasn't her one. He'd turned the corner, never to see the light of day again. Unled. No one helped him, and he blamed the Omegas, so he killed them.

I might feel bad for him under different circumstances.

I was sorry he'd had his heart broken, but tons of people did every day, and they didn't turn around and destroy everyone around them for having done so. If the guys had rejected me, I wouldn't have burned down the world. I'd have hurt, but somehow, I'd have come through the pain without ruining other people's entire existences. There were wolves who had died without ever getting to shift again because of the Accords.

He'd hated his life? Well, I was sorry to see that had happened to him. But sorry only went so far.

I'd pushed and pushed my energy into him, until he was almost healed. That wasn't going to be what happened here today. He just needed to un-Loup enough that Rainer could take out the Alpha in him. I let go, practically stumbling backwards. Strong hands grabbed me before I'd have fallen off the dock into the mud pit that was the lake.

But I wasn't quite done. "Hold on."

I swung my hand out, letting my claws take care of the last bit of tether he had on anyone. I'd gotten most of it earlier, but the little grasp he had left was gone. Swish.

"Rainer, he's all yours."

My Alpha mate tilted his head. He pointed at Ross who panted, his eyes clear as he glared at Rainer. Then Rainer pointed at him. "I'm sure there are some official words that should be spoken here. But since you took that upbringing from us, forced us in hiding, and killed my father, who might have told me what to do, I'm just going to have to tell you that I'm going to kill you, and I don't even feel bad about it. Consider yourself Alpha challenged."

Preston pulled me out of the way as Rainer shifted midstride into his wolf form. Ross did the same. He didn't look like a Loup. No, I'd cleared that madness, but he still smelled wrong. Maybe some people were born that way, maybe someone else could have helped him. A better Omega, or someone who hadn't taken so much pain from him.

I would somehow have to live without being the Mother Theresa of Omegas. Maybe the ones who came after me could afford to be selfless. I had to rid the world of this menace just so they could exist.

The two male wolves lunged at each other, growling. Blood sprayed, and I winced, hoping it wasn't Rainer's. Or at least, that not too much of it was Rainer's.

"He'll be fine." Preston tugged me back again. The whole band of wolves that we'd brought with us were there watching. What had happened to all those Loups? I didn't care right then. I'd deal with fallout if fallout came.

"That was a pretty good speech for him not knowing it," Miranda shook her head. "Pretty close."

Anton rocked back on his feet and shot her a look that said her commentary wasn't really wanted at that moment. I wondered if she understood him. Alpha or no Alpha, I wouldn't put it past Anton to shove her in the water if she got too distracting while his brother was fighting.

"I need to shift." I didn't think the words before I spoke them. I just suddenly knew them to be true.

Anton shook his head as Jarret spoke. "No. Only the Alphas are shifted during the challenge. That much I remember from hearing Gus and Cristian reminisce. We stand as humans. They're the only wolves that matter here right now." Jarret nuzzled my neck. "But we get it. We all want to shift, too. If you do, you might interfere, you might not be able to control yourself."

It was hard enough like this. I craved blood like I could practically taste it on my tongue.

Rainer lunged at Ross, a piece of fur missing on my mate's coat. That must have been the initial blood. But Ross was bloodied, too. And more so than Rainer. Next to me, Preston growled. He wasn't shifted, but he might as well have been. His eyes were wolf. Growls started everywhere. Isaac. Miranda. Gus. My mother. We were all wolves right then, even if we couldn't be on four legs.

Every snap, tear, and hit was all consuming to watch. Rainer lifted his gaze for a split second and caught my own. I smelled the cinnamon of his focus but something else was in there, too. Joy, it was like a spring day. I startled. I couldn't be reading that right.

"Is he..."

Jarret sighed. "Happy. Yes, he's happy."

I almost laughed, but that would have been inappropriate. They really were perfect for me, we were all seriously sick in the head. Anton rolled his eyes. Rainer was toying with Ross. I should win an award for resisting the urge to yell out that he should finish it already.

"There he goes," Preston whispered in my ear.

How did he know? It must be all the years of experience they had with one another when they'd been allowed to shift. Rainer pinned Ross to the ground before he tore out his throat. A howl sounded, odd from human mouths but effective just the same. I smiled. Yes, death. We'd defeated an enemy, and it was time for this man to be dead.

"You can shift now."

I registered Jarret's words as everyone around me shifted seemingly all at once. They rushed at the body, tearing at it until they soaked themselves in blood. Preston went. Anton.

Jarret. But I stood there. Much as I wanted to earlier, what I craved now was something different.

Rainer walked toward me, slowly. He shifted as he came in front of me. The change quickly healed him, and when he stood in front of me, he was as healthy looking as I'd ever seen him.

"You did it."

He nodded. "I did. Whoever belonged to him belongs to me now. If they choose to stay."

They would. Who wouldn't pick Rainer? I kissed him hard. Blood splattered against us, and I smiled. This was what life was supposed to be like. We were wolves. There was blood and gore sometimes. It was as natural as breathing.

That was when it hit me.

The voices. Ross had controlled the Loups and the female versions, who didn't make the physical change but lost their minds just the same. They were all freed, but they weren't okay. Killing Ross didn't make them better.

Only I could do that, and they were...everywhere.

Rainer grasped me against him. "I can feel your pain. It's bad."

"So nice not to be alone in it." I pressed my head against his chest. "Thank you for doing what you did."

"Well, you made him nice and easy to bring down. Like you tenderized the meat first."

I groaned, sort of loving and hating his description at the same time. "You're welcome."

"Now what do we do about what's happening to you?"

I knew the answer to that. "We take me home to the swamp, and we see if our new pack will help us make things right."

"They will. If they want to stay with me."

For a man who had once thought he wasn't an Alpha and had just taken out a sick Alpha, he was fitting into the role of leader quite easily. Like he'd just put on a coat he'd forgotten he had, but was tailored just for him.

My other three mates surrounded me. Anton stroked his finger down my face and throat, leaving a trail of blood there. I understood what he was doing. We all took place in this, and we needed to share the blood. My wolf approved.

CHAPTER 10

My body ached like someone had beaten me, but I'd spent the last week like that and I was getting surprisingly used to it. Amazing how I could learn to endure certain things by just being given enough time. I might even feel weird when I wasn't in pain anymore.

I swung back and forth on the porch swing Jarret installed for me the day before and watched the sun set over the swamp. It was so darn quiet. That was what I was noticing the most when I could think. People had left. Miranda took her pack, including my brother Agustin, and went back home. Others had stayed. They were going to buy up and renovate the broken houses that lined the swamp. Come back home and revitalize this place. That had been the dream. That was what I'd imagined could happen.

They were Rainer's now.

Others had left us to go help me. My brother Isaac. Their father Gus. My mother. I needed the broken brought to me. I couldn't go to everyone, so I had to have them brought to me. I dreamed of them, and then I woke up and gave instructions. When I'd been on my own, that had been so painful. Now, it was just one of those things I was used to. The daughters of the Omega I had met in New Orleans had warned me there would be pain.

But I was managing. And Rainer thought it would get better incrementally, until I was able to endure it.

The Omegas in my head were being quiet on the subject. They might even be gone entirely, sent to me for one purpose and floated off now that Ross had been dealt with. Ross...

Maybe the Omegas had left because I wasn't selfless enough. I doubted that. Not one of them had been selfless, and the one who'd rejected him had caused this whole mess. If there was a tallying taking place somewhere in the universe, I had to imagine I was doing better than that. I closed my eyes and listened to the sounds of the crickets. They loved to show up at sunset.

Anton was coming to me. I knew it without opening my eyes. I could feel him in my whole body. Opening my lids, I waited for a few seconds before he rounded the corner. I wasn't sure what he'd been doing all day, but he'd been missing. Usually, he was very close by, which I loved. But they'd been giving me lots of space today. Maybe they thought I needed some alone time, which I did, but I could be alone around them, too. It was a weird dynamic. Things were just better when they were there.

He touched my hand to his heart when he got close enough, and I smiled at him. "Where have you been all day?"

As an answer, he scooped me up. I yelped, and he grinned. Okay. We were going somewhere. I was going to pretend I felt fine. We'd gotten rid of Ross. I didn't want everything to be dour. Once we got the numbers down in terms of people who needed my help, I'd feel better alto-gether. It was just wait and see. No one had come back with a Loup yet.

We rounded the corner from the house and walked a distance away, until we came to a dock I wasn't sure I'd been to before. The trees hung low, the moss dipping down until it seemed like it created a shade around us. He'd laid out a blanket.

I grinned at him, giving it my best fake Southern accent. The guys had great ones, and if Anton could speak aloud, he would, too. I was sure of it. Mine was horrific, so I made it even more so just for fun. "Why, Mr. Harper, I think you want to have your wicked way with me out on this dock."

He nodded, setting me down on the blanket. The blanket made it pretty comfortable, but I would make love to Anton in the dirt if that was our only choice. This was downright romantic. And there was the littlest amount of danger because we could be spotted. I didn't mind if he didn't. It was funny, everyone's individual comfort zone with sex. Anton did not want to have sex with me at the same time as anyone else, but this he desired. For now, I desired what they desired, their hearts were my own.

I stroked my hand down the side of his beloved face. "I love you."

He kissed me, and I could taste the passion on his tongue, feel his adoration on his breath. Every touch of his hand on any piece of exposed skin spoke of his feelings for me, and I wanted to rub against it and never let the feeling go. The good news was that I didn't have to, ever. I could have it for the rest of my life. Maybe after, considering all of the things that I had seen lately.

He placed my hand over his heart, nuzzling down on my shoulder like he had from one of the first moments I'd known him. This was our thing. I closed my eyes and let myself feel it. Life had been a constant battle since I'd woken up in Gus' truck, but I'd still had moments like the one with Anton that had arguably changed my life. Something had woken up inside of me and said yes...this is right...when he'd put his head right there on that spot on my shoulder.

Anton raised his gaze, and we shared that moment. He could feel it too, remember what had been between us almost immediately. How did I know? I'd never be able to explain it. We could read each other. He didn't need my words either. Just my soul, and I was beyond happy to share it with him.

I reached for his shirt just as he did my own. We undressed each other draped in the touches of sunlight that managed to reach us through the overgrown trees covering the swamp and our dock. Even though this might soon belong to someone else, it would always be in my mind, now thought of as *our dock*.

Pressing my tongue into his mouth, I sighed and held on to him tighter so that he might not slip into oblivion where such perfect moments were bound to disappear to. He gripped me tighter, rubbing his hand down my back between where I arched slightly over the dock. But he didn't keep his hands there very long.

Anton wasted no time, he slipped a finger inside of me where I was sure he'd find me wet and wanting him. Any pain I'd felt earlier was forgotten. Anton was the cure to anything that was currently wrong with me, at least for now. My breasts felt heavy, and my nipples begged for attention. The same way that he could always know what I was thinking, he understood what I needed too. With one hand continuing to stroke my clit in easy circles, like he knew just how much pressure to give me to build this explosion ever so slowly, he bit down on my nipple.

Eventually, my need to touch him was more than I could handle. I had to. Right that second. I reached between us and stroked his cock, feeling it grow in my hand until it pressed hard against my leg. He was warm, wet, and wanting me. With my other hand grasped on his back, I started to pant. I needed more, so much more, and yet I didn't want to stop what I was doing. Even knowing the next moment would be as equally perfect as this one, I was desperate to never let it go.

Anton made the choice for me. He stilled my hand, but just to reposition himself so that he could be closer to me, push inside of me when he wanted. I might beg him to hurry up, I might plead, but he gave me no reason to do those things. Anton would always feel what I did, he'd know my desperation.

He shook his head before he flipped me over. I yelped, not ready or even expecting him to do that. Anticipation made me shake. He was up on his knees as he pulled me against his chest, moving my legs to straddle him before he pushed me down on his hard, waiting cock. I cried out at the invasion and loved it at the same time.

This was Anton, dominating me in the most pleasure-filled way. My chest rose and fell as I tried to catch my breath. But there was no way to think through this or breathe my way into toning this down. My need for control had no place here. I moved when he took my hips and made me. Over and over, he did that. In those minutes, I was entirely his. I existed just for him. And there was so much joy and ease to this. It couldn't last forever, I wouldn't want it to, but for now, I would be happy to do this forever.

How Anton wanted me, he could have me, because what

I needed, he always understood. We'd never been so fully connected, so completely one with another. I might even be feeling his pleasure wrapped up with my own. What did it matter whose it was? We were together, body and soul in this moment, and all I knew was that it was both too much and not enough. There was no amount of Anton that would ever be enough, that would ever satisfy how much I needed him.

I exploded around him as he emptied himself inside of me. Anton pulled me off of him, only to roll me over so I was back on the blanket on the dock, both of us breathing hard.

"I know." I managed to speak. Because I did. All the things he would say if he could, but that I could hear anyway. I'd always know.

———

I was feeling better, looser, and Anton had his arm around me as we walked back over to the house. "Do you think anyone saw us?"

He shook his head. No, he'd set that up and watched it all day. No one had come around that way. At least I now knew where he had been. Things were starting to add up. I grinned at him. "That dock is going to belong to someone else soon."

Anton lifted an eyebrow. Unless he bought the house it belonged to. I leaned against his shoulder. "Don't we own two houses that are falling apart already? How many do we need?"

I didn't want to collect broken houses, not when I had so many broken werewolves heading my way. There were only so many things I could commit to fixing at once.

He nodded. Yep, he understood.

My hands burned, and I stared down at them as the feeling surprised me. It looked like someone was here. Rainer strode out the back door. "Gus is back."

That was fast. Where had he gone? "Must have been close."

"Not so close. Gus drives like a lunatic."

I didn't remember that. I'd been really out of it, but maybe he'd been extra cautious with me.

"Bring him out."

Rainer cupped my cheek. "Her. This one's a woman."

That was a change. "Got it. Bring her out."

It looked like I was getting started. The sooner I began, the faster we could get to normalcy, whatever that was going to prove to be.

Rainer nodded, his gaze moving over my body, like he was checking to make sure I was sound before he actually did it. "Jarret will bring him here. Then how about we eat dinner? I'm cooking tonight."

He cooked every night. That was a real benefit of having a chef living in the same house, and the fact that he wasn't actually cooking professionally at the moment. He had all those skills and instincts, and nowhere to use it but at home for us. "Thanks."

"Yep. Jarret will be back soon." Rainer looked down at his phone. "I'm thinking about putting these people being brought here in the other house. Making it a way station, so to speak. We can't just keep kicking out Loups like we were doing before. We're actively getting them. We need somewhere for them to sleep and eat before we throw them out."

Like a B&B for those needing my assistance. "That's a good idea. You know there is a third option outside of the idea that they'll disappear."

He stared at me a moment. "They'll want to join."

"Yes." Anton let go of me to walk in the house. He turned as he approached the door and winked at me. Our time together hadn't fled for either of us, and he wanted me to know. I would wink back, but Rainer was having a serious conversation with me and that would be just downright rude. That was okay. Anton knew I was winking on the inside.

"I've asked Preston to do a real strong look at the area and what we can acquire real estate wise and what we can't. There are humans who might want to be bought out, but we have to be careful. I'd love to have what Miranda has, an entirely werewolf town. We should always have had that. They can defend and protect better." He ran a hand through his hair. "And we'll have to start charging a monthly pack association fee like my father used to so we can assist any people who can't afford to buy, we can rent out to them. So many people won't have anything. The world was taken from us."

People were going to show up soon who had been under the control of Ross. They were going to be lost and confused. They might not know how much time had even passed. My guess was they'd find their way here, too. We were going to be a destination of choice for a while, and some of them might stay permanently. They might be our pack.

But one thing at a time, really. All we could handle was who showed up now and what they needed. One moment at a time.

Preston snored next to me when the bed dipped, Jarret coming to join us. I knew it was him without having to open my eyes. My wolf senses were really the best thing. He wrapped his arms around me, joining Preston's from the other side, and I smiled.

"Hey." It was still dark outside. It must still be night. That much I could garner without really having to open my eyes. It didn't have the feel of daytime yet.

"Hey back." He kissed my neck where my hair exposed it and settled in. I loved this part of our life. The ease with which we got to simply be who we were. They came and went from my bed, and I always had someone to hold me. I hadn't known how much I needed it, people to care, but now that I'd had it, I could never do without it.

And my mates were really cuddly. They might hate anyone knowing it, so that would just be my secret.

Preston snored on, deep in dreamland, and since I'd come to associate the sound with him, I really didn't mind listening to the rhythmic breathing, and I let it lull me into my own deep sleep.

I walked forward through snow, barefoot as I always was in these vision dreams, but I didn't feel the cold. Snowflakes bit my cheeks, but it wasn't uncomfortable, more like someone tickled me.

I never saw who I was there to visit right away. I always had to walk to them, as though it was a choice I was making. That wasn't true. This happened whether I wanted it to or not, and it hurt. Sometimes they showed me monstrous things, but it always passed, and when it was over, I knew I had to send someone to them and where they were. That was a real gift in the midst of the painfulness of my role.

Ross being gone didn't mean that the problems of being an Omega were lessened. They would be with me forever, always my burden. I could fight against it, or find a way to breathe through it. Or at least, that was what I told myself in these moments when I struggled.

I wasn't really here. I was in bed with Preston and Jarret snuggling me. They wouldn't know this was happening until I jerked awake and disturbed their sleep. Not that they complained.

That was when I saw the Loup in front of me. He was a fully formed Loup in the deep stages of his madness. Probably, he'd belonged to Ross, and now he would be mine, until I set him free.

"Help." His words were the deep guttural mumblings of a wrongly formed wolf. Just another indecency thrust upon him by this strange existence so many of our people had to endure.

"I can." I nodded. "But I'm not really here with you, and you are far from me. I'm going to send someone to you to help you. If you can control yourself, I don't want you to hurt them. They are there for me. If you can't, they'll subdue you. You want to try not to have that happen." I was never sure if they understood me. I said it anyway because that way, I knew that I had. I could at least always try to do the right thing. "Where are you?"

He blinked. They could usually grasp that much in our conversation. Otherwise, I was going to have to look for clues and ask my family to help me find them like they had with Ross. We were people seekers, and thank the universe for the Internet and a total lack of privacy anywhere. Anyone could be found, it seemed, if we knew how to investigate.

"I'm outside of Vail."

I sucked in a breath. "That's where I was from. In Colorado."

"I know." The Loup blinked rapidly, and realization

dawned on me. I knew who he was, just as he knew me. I'd never have recognized him, and I should have because he was my brother. We'd been waiting for my family to return, and now I knew at least why Caleb hadn't. He'd been lost to us, connected to Ross for the time we'd all been missing, like this. Tears flooded my eyes.

"There you are."

I jolted up in bed, and the tears I'd cried in my sleep followed me to wakefulness in big, heaving gulps of air.

Preston tugged me to him, strong arms to take the pain, with Jarret quickly behind me, placing gentle kisses on my shoulder blades.

"Bad one?" he asked me between kisses. "They're not usually quite so awful. Tell me."

Preston said sweet things in my ear. How much he loved me, how it was all going to be okay. I had to tell them, because truly, there wasn't a second to be lost.

"My brother."

They both went still for a second before Preston got up on his knees, letting me go. "Tell me where he is, and I'll be there tomorrow."

"Home. He's close to home. My old home. Outside of Vail."

Preston pushed the covers off the bed on his way getting up, and Jarret followed him. I guessed they were both going. The younger one smiled at me, a small movement of his lips that didn't show any joy. It was meant to be comforting, and I appreciated the effort.

"We won't let anything happen to him."

I crab walked to the end of the bed and took their hands. They'd not gone to collect anyone for me before, but it was right to send them now. Both my mother and Isaac were out already. Every wolf I helped was important, but this was my brother. I couldn't help it, and maybe it was nepotism. I wasn't going to overthink it. I did want it to be Preston and Jarret who went to get him.

"Thank you."

Rainer strode through the door. "What's going on?" He rubbed at his eyes. "I...I smelled distress."

Anton pushed through, also obviously having just woken up.

"She saw her brother. He's a Loup. We're going."

Rainer nodded once before he opened his arms, and I walked into them. It was good to have mates. Anton hugged around both of us. Really, really good.

"His name is Caleb. And he's a dreamer. He's the one who wanted to go do great things. Save the world. Sail the oceans in a small boat he commanded himself. Find a human girl he could actually love, and somehow make our lives during the Accords work. And now there he is, lost in the snow."

Rainer sucked in a breath. "He's not lost, because you found him. That's what you do, MacKenzie Harper, you find lost souls and you bring them home again. You'll be his miracle, just like you are for the rest of us."

———

It was somehow easier when we had a bad guy to fight. I thought that ridiculous thing as I swung on the porch again. Not that Ross was a bad guy like out of a comic book or something. Well, maybe he was. I didn't really know what he'd been, but he had been something for me to fight, to find, even to flee. Now here I was without anything to battle but time, and that was not a war I was going to win.

I had to wait.

The humans said patience was a virtue. My wolf and I were in agreement. It fucking sucked, and I didn't feel anything was particularly virtuous about it.

I'd fixed a wolf today, but he wasn't my brother. The man —his name was Jesse—had a family, some of whom were here. The rest weren't accounted for yet. There were a lot of lost souls. Jesse and one of his daughters were in Rainer's B&B—he hated that name for it—and now I was once again without something to do.

Except swing.

Rainer came out the backdoor. "MacKenzie, come with me, please. I'd like to show you something."

I ached, but that wasn't going to be better or worse for going with him, so I quickly followed him to his car. "Where are we going?"

He winked at me as Anton had done the day before, and then he grinned. Had he known that had happened? I wouldn't have been surprised. Rainer did seem to know things that were going on, even if he didn't comment on them. I loved learning things about them every day.

"You'll find out."

It was the first time I'd been in the car since we'd gotten back. It was much nicer than being in the RV, and I much preferred it. Rainer rolled down the window, and we let the wind strike at us as he drove us to some unknown destination he had yet to tell me about. I chewed on my lip. It wasn't possible my brother would get there in the time we were away. It was going to take them a bit to locate him, and they'd call on their way back.

I was allowed to do this. I had to remember that. Much as I was going to live for others, there had to be moments for me.

CHAPTER 11

We left town and drove several miles more, until he pulled off the road to an empty building that had seen better days. But then again, every building I looked at lately had that same situation. Everything needed someone to take the time to fix it. And I supposed we had nothing but time right now, which was a gift but felt off after running for so long.

Did it ever feel natural to slow down?

We were wolves, we liked to run, but we also craved pack, home, family. The dichotomy of our lives never ceased to amaze me.

"What am I looking at?

The bones of the building were pretty, like a log cabin.

"I think I'm going to fix this place up and open a restaurant."

I gasped. "Rainer, really?"

"Good idea or bad idea? I'm not doing it without your approval."

Well, that was a heavy thing to take on. "I don't know if I'm the person to tell you what to do. I have no future plans except, I guess, being the Omega. But this is a great spot. It's right off the highway. I don't know the area that well yet, but if we're going to revitalize it by becoming a wolf area, then I imagine people will come to eat."

He was talented, made delicious food. Plus, he loved it. And it wouldn't hurt he was Alpha. It probably was a good thing for business.

Rainer leaned against one of the poles outside. "You have a good eye. Can you see a restaurant here?"

I stepped inside the building and looked around. There was a kitchen, albeit not much of one at the moment, in the back. This place had been a restaurant before. I spun around. Yes, I could see people seated, I could see this functioning. Laughter. Good food. The occasional glare at a human who found their way here, since it was a wolf place, even if they didn't know it. Rainer's stories at the end of the night. A real look of satisfaction on his face when he came home from doing it.

"Yes, it could work. It should. This is your place."

He stepped toward me, taking a strand of my hair in his fingers. "Ours."

My cheeks warmed. "That will take some getting used to."

Rainer drew me to him. He was warm, solid, and strong. "I know." He kissed my neck. "It's hard. Like it's going to irk me to ask Preston for the loan. He'll probably try to just give it to me. We'll have a thing. But at the end of the day, I'll take it and be grateful. He won't understand what the big deal is, because what is his is mine. And eventually, we'll all settle into the idea that it works that way."

I leaned against him. "Look at you being all wise. Is it an Alpha thing?"

"You know how you changed when you really started to

feel like the Omega you already were? It's happening to me. I saw one of the wolves who stayed today. He was downtown opening a bank account, and I thought...I should really tell him about the hardware store two towns from here. Like I am suddenly consumed with the happiness of the people who are staying."

That made sense. They were his now. Like they were mine. "They need to Alpha swear to you."

"We'll get to it." His voice lowered. "I'm going to pick you up." That was the only warning I got before he did just that. "This place is dirty. I'm not touching you here. But I always want you, so I'm going to put you in the car and take you someplace else."

I smiled at him. "You've gotten my approval, and now you want my approval in...other things."

His smile could only be called wolfish, which was somehow appropriate, considering all things. When he'd shut me in the car, I leaned over and unlocked the door for him. These were old vehicles. We still had to be considerate of each other. When he'd gotten inside, I climbed right on top of him. "Push the seat back as far as you can."

Rainer's eyes widened. "Here?"

"Why not?" I felt almost wicked propositioning him to have sex with me in the middle of the day in a car on the side of a road where anyone could see. But I wanted him. Now.

His eyes turned wolf before they returned quickly back to his human form. "Why not? Good answer."

He kissed me, running his tongue over my lips. I shivered, wanting more but not wanting to rush it either. "I wish you could see all the ways that you've changed." He kissed me gently all over my face. Then he moved down to my neck. We didn't have a huge amount of space to move like this. That was fine. We weren't going to need it. "You were lost when you came to us, and now you are filled up to the brim with light and purpose. You brighten everyone's existence, and we're all better to have known you, let alone to get to love you."

"Oh, Rainer..." Tears flooded my eyes, cutting me off. He changed his kisses, harder and more demanding, not seeming to be bothered by the fact that he'd made me cry. I quickly ceased, my attention moving from his sweet words to the way that he was kissing me.

I pulled his shirt over his head and threw it onto the passenger seat. We weren't going to be able to get totally naked in this car, but I wanted to touch his skin with my skin. I loved how Rainer looked shirtless. Maybe that was some kind of cliché, being really attracted to the sharp draw of his abdomen, the way he seemed like he'd been built out of stone. I loved to touch him.

Despite the awkwardness of the fact that I could end up accidentally beeping the horn of the car or hitting some gear, I took the time to touch him, just to watch the way that his muscles jumped under my caress. He flared his nostrils. The scent in the car was heady. Even in my human form, I could scent the smell of arousal filling the small space. It was sweet, and not something I could say was relatable to any other smell out there. It was just Rainer and me.

"MacKenzie, those fingers of yours are going to be my undoing."

I could do better than my hands. "We have to slip out of pants."

Rainer sort of grunted more than answered me. We both started to pull at our clothes. He finally lifted his head to stare at me as I pulled mine off. "Next time, we're going to do this slowly, and I'm going to get my fill of your breasts."

Sounded like a plan. His cock was hard, and I rubbed against it for a second. I was wet with wanting him, and all we'd really done was kiss. But I was always going to want him like this.

I fitted him inside of me. He moaned, throwing his head back. Every nerve ending in my body came to life. Yes, I wanted this, needed the release that only Rainer could give me. I was going to have to do all the moving. He was all but pinned on this seat. Up and down, I rode his cock as best I could. At this angle, I could rub him against my clit with every pass. It was sweet torture. I put my hands on the ceiling of the car, my knees digging into the seat and possibly Rainer's thigh as I dug down and thrust up. We joined each other in crying out at the same time, as though we were making music.

He squeezed my breasts through my clothes. Over and over, the minutes passed. He grew inside of me, and my movements were stilted. We were both panting, sweaty, wet, and I was still half-dressed. It wouldn't be the most glamorous of views if someone were looking. I smiled at the thought and came hard. My explosion of pleasure must have triggered his own. We came together before I fell on top of him completely, his strong hands holding me up while I let the pleasure still riding me rush me away into a euphoria I'd be happy to never leave again.

———

Rainer squeezed my hand as we walked back into our house. Our clothes were a mess. If anyone wanted to comment, they'd know exactly what we'd done. Not that any of my mates would comment, and only Anton was home. I could smell him in his office writing. His scent made me smile. It was so nice to have people to come home to.

And equally as nice to have someone to come with. This really was home, even if it was broken and needed some tender loving care, very soon. Some furniture, too.

"You should enroll in school here." Rainer kissed my cheek. "You know you want to."

I'd hardly let myself think about it. I dropped my gaze from Rainer. In this moment, it felt more like he was my Alpha giving me direction than one of the loves of my life.

"Don't look away." He tipped my chin. "If I'm wrong, tell me so."

He wasn't, that was the thing. "How can I? I don't have the slightest idea what to do with my life."

Rainer kissed my cheek again. "That's what people go to college to find out, right? You don't have to have all your information just yet. You're incredibly smart. You'll figure it out."

I sighed. "Can I though? Isn't what I'm going to do pretty much have to revolve around being the Omega?"

"I have no idea what the previous Omegas did and didn't do in terms of jobs. Do you?" He walked into the kitchen, and I followed after him. Why did Rainer think this was so simple?

I didn't have an answer to his question. "They're not in my head anymore, so no."

"Even if they were all just preoccupied being Omegas, if it took over their lives, that doesn't mean that has to be you. We make our own rules." He scooted up on the counter as his phone dinged. Rainer pulled it out of his pocket. "They're on their way back with your brother."

Excitement filled me. That was a very good thing. Okay. I took a deep breath. "Good."

"If you don't want to go, don't go to school. It's a thought. That's all."

The thing was he was right. I did want to go to college. "How will I pay for it?"

Anton knocked on the wall. He must have been listening, and I'd been too distracted to notice he was there. He was going to pay for my schooling.

"That's good." Rainer nodded. "He can pay for your school, and I'll borrow from Preston. In five years, we can all be set up and I won't have to beg from my little brothers."

Anton threw a towel at him, and Rainer laughed. "See? I told you, MacKenzie. It's uncomfortable, but they don't even seem to mind."

My mates were everything. Anton came up behind me and held me close. His breath on my shoulder was comforting, not sexual in that moment. This was reassurance. He wanted to send me to school. He had the means. Why was I giving it a second thought?

"Okay. Thank you. I'll go to school. And figure out something that makes me happy in between being the only Omega alive."

Rainer laughed, throwing his head back. "Yep. Just that small, unimportant role. If anyone can do it, MacKenzie, you can."

———

They arrived in the middle of the night, bringing my brother in a cage with them. Jarret hugged me close. "Sorry about the cage. He wasn't happy to see us."

Loups never were, and despite a little coherence in our shared dream, it wasn't unusual for him to have no idea what was happening when approached. "How badly did he fight you?"

"Nothing we couldn't handle, Mac." Preston strode through the door. "And we managed not to hurt him, I think."

The Loups never spoke of pain. Their whole lives were pain. My mother would be back soon. My other brother. I didn't want them to find him like this. It was hard enough that I had to see it, and I could give them this, at least. When they got back, they'd have him back, looking like he should and on his way to recovery.

"Do you need to eat something?" Rainer stepped up behind me.

It was a valid question, but I was already in the zone. I wrapped my arms around my brother and held on. It occurred to me something that I'd known and forgotten as things had gone askew. This was my brother, but every wolf I helped had been someone's something at some point. That was vague, but it was true. We all should have had a pack. We should have mattered, and that had been ripped away from us. Every time I did this, it brought pack the possibility of reuniting a family. Of a pack forming somewhere. Or even the chance that they might be my pack now.

This was my brother, but he might someday leave me to go off on his own or find a mate like Agustin did and choose a different pack. That made me sad but also happy for him, because that was what we had now, choices.

We were werewolves, and no one would take that from us again. I would see to that.

My brother's pain filled me, and tears came to my eyes. I held on to him because he belonged to me, but also for all the brothers, sisters, daughters, sons, friends, and werewolf brethren who ever lived and ever would be.

I was an Omega.

It was what we did.

"Oh no." My mother's voice flooded my consciousness. "Is that Caleb? My baby."

I held on tighter.

The moon was full, and I ran through the swamp chasing Jarret. I followed my nose. There was a fox nearby, and it would be mine. I would see to it. That was prey, and I was a hunter. Right now, nothing mattered but getting that fox.

With my nose to the ground, I just kept running. A wolf ran out in front of me, and I skidded to a stop. Preston stood there, and he made a slight growling noise in his throat. What was the problem? I watched where he looked and saw the alligator. Oh, I'd missed that. I'd gotten so used to their smells around when we were running. The gators were always there, and I'd not realized it was so close.

I wasn't the best wolf when it came to hunting with my nose. But I would get better. My competitiveness had gone nowhere. It came with me, regardless of what form I was in.

He nudged me left, and I ran with him, following Jarret again. Rainer stood next to a tree on two feet. He'd been taking Alpha pledges all day. I guessed he had found us. Spotting us running, he shifted and charged toward us. I smiled. Let him catch me. I took off running, passing Jarret, who huffed his displeasure and ran to catch up. Anton was a distance ahead. He swung around, his head tilted in question, but he caught on soon. All four of them chased me. That was okay. I could do this all fucking day.

I was pretty darn fast when I was running at top speed.

There was so much freedom in this. The Accords had taken this, and we had fought to get it back.

This was mine. I was the Omega, and I had the four most incredible mates in the universe. Anyone who came after us was going to have to come through me.

I dared them to try.

There was so much freedom in this. I had... I had taken... ...to a length of... ...both...
This was only... ...was it... ...to do... ...and I had... ...four... ...was... going... ...so... ...
hard... ...to try...

EPILOGUE

My psych textbook was heavy, dense, and wonderful. There was nothing I loved to study more than psychology. I didn't know if I could make a career out of it, but I loved spending the time to learn what the professor assigned and then extra just for fun.

I'd never have imagined I'd like this, but maybe it had something to do with all the things I had seen in the last year.

The house smelled like scallops. Rainer was trying a recipe here he would use at work next week. I loved Sundays. We were all home. Anton walked by and kissed my cheek, but otherwise didn't bother me. They were used to me studying a lot, and I'd never had so much support in my life.

My phone blew up. My mother wanted dinner this week, and my mother-in-law was pregnant and wanted me to see her ultrasound. I think what everyone wanted was to know when I was going to have a baby. The answer was that I hoped to do that after I had a career going. Whatever that was going to look like. I hoped that was five to six years from now. I'd be about twenty-eight years old.

As we lived a long time with an extended fertility, I didn't see any problem with waiting that long.

Jarret was covered in paint. He sat on the porch humming to himself next to Preston, who was talking on the phone about some obnoxious customer they'd had that day. He was assuring the person on the phone that they, as the employee, had done nothing wrong.

These were the sounds I loved, the smells I'd never stop adoring, and the way it was for us as a family.

The sound of a car pulling down the driveway surprised me. Our house was mostly done, but no one came to visit us unannounced. Rainer was big on that. Unless there was an emergency, we were available by appointment.

Loups were an emergency, but they were few and far between these days. I was the only Omega, but my schedule had eased considerably.

Rainer strode from the kitchen out the front door. He'd deal with whoever it was. I looked back down at my textbook. I could do this electronically, but I loved this paper book. Still, I couldn't seem to manage to pull my attention away from the low spoken conversation outside. Okay. I had to go see who was there.

I strode through the door as Jarret opened it for me.

"Kenzie, I think you'd better come."

I was already there. I squeezed his arm on the way out to the porch. The sounds of our swamp hit me hard as I exited. I loved it here.

A woman and a man I'd never seen before stood on the driveway. They held a baby.

Preston met my gaze. "This is crazy."

What was crazy? I could ask, but instead, I strode

forward towards our guest. Rainer wasn't worried, or I'd never have gotten this far. The woman had dark circles under her eyes, and the man had a protective arm around her.

"Omega?" Her voice was low. "I'm sorry to bother you, but we didn't know where to go."

"I'm glad you came." I didn't really know what they wanted yet, but...then I smelled it. The baby. They were here for her. She was very young, a few weeks old. And her scent...I knew it.

Omega.

"We were afraid, hiding. Our people were going missing, and then that stopped thanks to you. That's what we heard." The man spoke. "Our daughter. She smells...well, we think she's an Omega. We don't know what to do. We've only been shifting again for a little while, and what does someone do for an Omega? Only you would know."

Only I would know. I stared at the dark brown hair on the sleeping infant and let her scent move through me. Well there it was. Ross was gone. We'd won. And there she was. An infant.

An Omega.

I wasn't alone.

I never would be again. "Come inside. I think we have much to talk about."

———

AFTERWORD

Thank you so much for reading Caught! I hope you loved The Swamp series and will consider leaving it a review! If you like werewolf romances, I'd love for you to try out some more of mine. I have three series that feature werewolves, two of which are complete.

Please try the Westervelt Wolves: https://amzn.to/39CSuV6

Please try The Fallen Alphas: https://amzn.to/3fcE4wo

Please try The Dragon Wars: https://amzn.to/30fNLG9

Or turn the page to learn more about my 100+ books!

Thanks!
RR

Please Turn the page for a complete list of my books

ABOUT THE AUTHOR

As a teenager, I would hide in my room to read my favorite romance novels when I was supposed to be doing my homework.

I am the mother of three adorable boys and I am fortunate to be married to my best friend. I live in Austin Texas where I am determined to eat all the barbecue in town.

I am in love with science fiction, fantasy, and the paranormal and try to use all of these elements in my writing. I've been told I'm a little bloodthirsty so I hope that when you read my work you'll enjoy the action packed ride that always ends in romance. I love to write series because I love to see characters develop over time and it always makes me happy to see my favorite characters make guest appearances in other books.

In my world anything is possible, anything can happen, and you should suspect that it will.

I'd love to hear from you! Please visit my website at www.rebeccaroyce.com to sign up for my newsletter and learn about my books!

Here's where you can find me online:

Rebecca's Randomness Reading Group https://www.facebook.com/groups/RebeccasRandomness/

https://www.rebeccaroyce.com

https://www.facebook.com/authorrebeccaroyce/

www.twitter.com/rebeccaroyce

Instagram: rebeccaroyce79
Cheers!!
Rebecca

Tradition Be Damned

Past Be Damned

Destiny Be Damned

Compassion Be Damned

Future Be Damned

Dragon Wars (completed series)

Forever

Eternal

Always

Evermore

Endless

Wards and Wands (completed series)

Hexed and Vexed

Curse Reversed

Meow, Baby (novella, co-written with Ripley Proserpina)

Tragic Magic

Safe Haven

Everywhere and Nowhere

Dimension X (coming soon)

More coming soon....

Soul Bound

Prisoner of the Dragons

More coming soon....

Shadow Promised

Strange Days

Weird Nights

Bizarre Years

More coming soon...

The Warrior (completed series)

Initiation

Driven

Subversive

Redemption

Justice

Warrior World (spin off of The Warrior, completed series)

Deacon

Micah

Jason

The Westervelt Wolves (completed series)

Her Wolf

Summer's Wolf

Wolf Reborn

Wolf's Valentine

Wolf's Magic

Alpha Wolf

Angel's Wolf

Darkest Wolf

Lone Wolf

Fallen Alpha

Alpha Rising

Alpha's Strength

Alpha's Sacrifice

Alpha's Truth

Alpha Enticing

Hidden Alpha (coming soon)

Illicit Minds

Illicit Senses

Illicit Connections

Illicit Alliance (coming soon)

The Outsiders

Love Beyond Time

Love Beyond Sanity

Love Beyond Loyalty

Love Beyond Sight

Love Beyond Expectations

Love Beyond Oceans

Love Beyond Flames

Love Beyond Lies

Love Beyond Death (coming soon)

Cascade (completed series)

Haunted Redemption

Phoenix Everlasting

Fragility Unearthed

Persuasion Enraptured

Reverse Harem Story (completed series)

Unconventional

Unexpected

Undeniable

Kiss Her Goodbye (completed series)

Hard Truths

Dark Truths

Deadly Truths

Shifter World

Planet Bear

Planet Wolf (coming soon)

The Swamp

Hidden

Pursued

Caught

Stand Alone Titles

Under The Lights

No Quitting Allowed

Mr. Wrong

Bite Marks

Bitten Surrender

The Vampire and The Virgin

Demon Within

Crimson Lust

Call Me Crazy

The Men of Elite Metal

The Storm (writing with Ripley Proserpina) **completed series.**

Lightning Strikes

Thunder Rolling

The Deluge

Heart of the Nebula (writing with Heather Long) **completed series**

Queenmaker

Deal Breaker

Throne Taker

Stupid Boys (writing with C.R. Jane)

Stupid Boys

Dumb Girl

Crazy Love

Through the Gates (writing with Skye MacKinnon)

Purgatory City

Infernal Land

The Coveted (writing with Ripley Proserpina)

Eyes in the Darkness

Voices in the Darkness

Return to the Darkness

Prison Princess (part of the Prison Princess world, writing with CoraLee June)